SUMMERS SLAIN

A LADY GAYLE SUMMER MYSTERY

CASSIE RUSH

Published: April 2023

Gordian Knot Publishing

Paperback ISBN: 978-1-913948-05-4

Created with Vellum

CONTENTS

CHAPTER
ONE

Lady Gayle Summer flinched as the motor car behind her backfired. She brushed the ochre dust from the portico pillar off her heavy, black coat as she followed her mother up the short flight of steps into the hallway of Bethencourt Castle.

Making a mental note to discuss the smooth running of the Bentley's engine with Chadwick, the chauffeur—after all, she had been a mechanic and ambulance driver during the Great War—she began to unbutton her new winter coat. Then she frowned, and thinking she might forget, she decided to mention the noise to Chadwick immediately. She marched towards the entrance as the butler, Fredericks, began closing the front door. Below on the gravel drive, Chadwick was on the point of leaping back into the Bentley to start the engine. Odd, she thought, something must have backfired, but what? She pursed her lips and glanced up at Fredericks, nodding at him to shut the door. Still frowning, she shrugged off her coat and handed it and the black cloche hat to Alice, her maid and onetime war comrade.

Alice bobbed a curtsy. 'Will that be all, milady?'

Lady Gayle nodded. 'I think I'll spend some time taking care of Mama before Mr Southall arrives. We won't bother dressing for dinner this evening.'

'Very good, milady.' Alice shook the coat and a nugget of ochre-coloured plaster fell to the floor. She swooped down to collect it, but although on the point of popping it in her apron pocket, she placed it in Lady Gayle's outstretched hand.

Lady Gayle frowned at the lump of ochre plaster for a moment, rolling it around in the palm of her hand. *Where on earth can that have come from?* She looked upwards, but the tawny lump did not match the ceiling. However, with a swift raise of her shoulders, she dismissed the puzzle, popped the plaster into her handbag and joined her mother in the drawing room.

Her mother, Lady Ethel Summer, the Countess Bethencourt, was already seated on a sofa facing the fire, back ramrod straight. She wound a delicate, black-trimmed, lace handkerchief around her fingers as she stared into the flames. The mismatched pack of dogs lay in front of the fire, heads on paws and letting out the occasional whimper.

'Would you like tea, Mama?' Lady Gayle asked, looking around for the bell rope.

'Something stronger, I think,' replied her mother. 'Especially since we have to endure the Gosforths for dinner this evening.'

Lady Gayle glanced at the Louis XV carriage clock on the mantel over the fire. It was scarcely past lunchtime and unlike her mother to indulge in alcohol this early in the day, but then when were funerals ordinary days? 'Dash it all,' she said. 'I'd forgotten about the Gosforths. Why did we invite them again?'

Her mother didn't reply but dabbed her eyes with the

handkerchief. Lady Gayle felt a rush of sympathy. After all, it wasn't every day you put your husband in the ground, she thought.

She strolled to the drinks trolley and poured her mother a small gin. After a moment's hesitation, she poured one for herself too. Although it was four years since she'd buried her own husband—who died from his war wounds—today had brought back a raft of painful memories.

Having handed her mother the drink, she wandered to the tall windows which gave out over the parkland of Bethencourt Castle. Gaspod, her late father's enormous bloodhound, followed her, and she stroked his soft, silky ears as the dog leaned against her legs. Outside, the lawns ran downhill to a lake where she and her brother, Alfred, had played on their sporadic visits to Great Uncle Percival as children. She allowed herself a moment's relief in happy memories before dragging herself back to the present and the vast changes that had occurred in their lives since the war and again in recent months.

When Great Uncle Percival died in the spring, leaving the estate and title to her father, she gained a title. Having been the Honourable Gayle Summer all her life, she was now Lady Gayle Summer. For a long time, she'd wondered if she'd ever get used to it. Now her father too had died after a fall from his horse, and the estate would be handed to someone else. If only her brother had survived the war, she thought, then the estate would have gone to him. *Whoever it is, I wish them luck. There has been so much death in recent years.*

'I'm sorry,' she said, turning towards her mother. 'I didn't hear you.'

'What time will the solicitor be here?' Her mother repeated her question and took another sip from her glass.

'Soon. He had to collect the will from his safe.'

'Such a nuisance; he should have brought it with him to the church.' Countess Bethencourt finished her gin and stared meaningfully at her daughter.

'I think there were several documents, Mama.' Lady Gayle turned away from the view, wondering once more who would inherit the title and the castle now. At least she could return to her life and friends in London. *I can't wait.*

There was a gentle knock on the door and a polite cough as the butler entered. 'Mr Southall has arrived. I've put him in the library, my lady.'

'Very well,' replied the countess. She pushed herself to her feet, flapping away her daughter's attempts to assist. 'I am perfectly capable of walking to the library, Gayle. Don't make a fuss.' The countess glided across the rugs, the hem of her black dress brushing the floor as she passed. Lily, her tiny Yorkshire Terrier, closely followed her passage from the room.

Lady Gayle smoothed the skirt of her drop-waisted dress, ensuring her knees were covered, and followed her mother. The countess abhorred modern fashions and wasted no opportunity to share her views with her daughter.

The solicitor, Mr Southall, had made himself comfortable at the only desk in the library. Lady Gayle snatched a glance at her mother on hearing the sharp intake of breath. Since they had taken up residence in the castle a few short months beforehand, the desk had been her father's domain. Seeing another man sitting in his place brought the grief into sharp focus.

Lady Gayle followed her mother to a pair of sofas which faced each other by the fire. Only by sitting next to each other could they both keep the solicitor in their line of vision. As already requested, Fredericks brought in tea, although Lady Gayle noticed he had refreshed her mother's gin and added a little ice. The countess sipped and held the glass on her lap. Glancing down, Lady Gayle could not help but notice her mother gripping the glass. The older woman's knuckles grew whiter as she clenched the crystal.

She's as worried as I am. What is to become of us?

Lady Gayle turned her gaze to Mr Southall as he shuffled papers on the desk as if he were awaiting orders.

'Do make a start, man,' commanded the countess. 'Or we shall be here all night. I would like to rest before dinner.'

'By all means, Countess,' the little man replied. He pushed his wire-rimmed spectacles up his nose and regarded them both.

Lady Gayle bit her lip, holding on to irreverent mirth, when she spotted his watery blue eyes, enlarged by the thick spectacle lenses. *He looks as innocent as a child.*

'As you are aware, Earl Cedric Bethencourt recently inherited the castle, the title, the estate and fortune from his cousin, the late Earl Percival Bethencourt—'

'That would be his first cousin once removed,' interrupted the countess. 'Percival and Cedric shared a *great*-grandfather, not a grandfather.' The countess took a large sip of her gin. The level in the glass had dropped with a dangerous swiftness.

'I encouraged him to make a will, which I am happy to report he did,' continued Mr Southall as if the interruption had not occurred. 'Earl Cedric Bethencourt leaves a few annuities to his staff, the staff here at Bethencourt Castle having already been adequately provided for in the late Lord Percival's will. There is also a provision for yourself, Countess, but the majority of his earlier inheritance and the title has been left to Lady Gayle Summer, or should I say Countess Bethencourt?'

'That's preposterous,' the older countess exclaimed. 'The estate has been entailed. My daughter can inherit nothing.'

'Countess, or should I say, Dowager Countess, the entailment was for twelve generations. Your late husband was the last of those generations and was free to leave his estate to whomsoever he chose. Since his son was killed in the Great War, he chose his daughter.'

The solicitor switched his watery gaze to Lady Gayle. 'You, my lady, are now Countess Bethencourt,' he said. 'The castle and the entire estate are for you to do with as you will, apart from selling it. That is one stipulation of your father's will. You may not sell the estate.'

The new Countess Bethencourt brushed a tear from her cheek. 'I don't know what to say,' she said. 'I expected to be told who the new earl would be and how soon we should be asked to leave.'

'There is no one else,' said Mr Southall sadly. 'Although—'

'Well, either there is someone or there isn't,' said the Dowager Countess. 'Spit it out, Mr Southall. Don't keep us in suspense.'

'Your late husband and I had heard of a child. A boy. But despite all efforts, he has not been found. In any case, Lord Cedric inherited as was his right, and he willed the property to his daughter as, once more, was his right. The boy, should such a person exist, would be entitled to the property only if something were to happen to the current Countess Bethencourt. Since she is a young lady of a robust disposition, that is hardly likely to happen for some time.'

'What happens to me?' The new Dowager Countess's voice shook and took on a querulous tone.

'Nothing, Mama. Nothing will change. You'll live here with me, and we will carry on as before.'

'Don't be ridiculous, child, you know nothing of running an estate like this,' replied her mother. 'How on earth will you manage? How will any of us manage without your dear papa?'

Lady Gayle rose, and Mr Southall jumped to his feet. 'I am not a child, Mama,' she said.

'Indeed, you are not. We must find you another husband, and you will produce an heir. There will be no more talk of alternative heirs.'

'Mother, I have no plans to find a new husband. Even if there were anyone suitable left.' Lady Gayle sighed. She bit her lip and dropped her gaze to her stomach where her hand rested lightly. Her own husband had been one of the many young men lost during the Great War.

She raised her chin, pulling back her shoulders. 'I played my part during the war, Mama, and if that experience taught me anything, it taught me that I am perfectly capable of learning anything I choose to.'

CHAPTER TWO

Dowager Countess Bethencourt stared at her daughter. 'I never approved of you being a mechanic,' she said. 'All that oil and grime. Not to mention the state of your hands. Most unladylike.' Suddenly, she rose and stepped swiftly from the room with her little dog, Lily, hard on her heels. Fredericks only had just enough time to reach the door to open it for them as the dowager, in high dudgeon, and dog swept through the doorway.

'If you would sit again, Countess,' said Mr Southall. 'There are a few matters that I would like to address with you as a matter of urgency.'

Lady Gayle glanced at the closing door and then at Fredericks' impassive face. *Gosh, if only people were as easy to deal with as engines.* She slumped onto the sofa with none of her mother's Victorian grace. 'Very well,' she said, 'but I think I must spend some time with my mother. She is very distraught as you saw. She rarely lets anyone see how upset she is. Bad manners, she always told me.'

'I would not ask if it were not urgent,' murmured Mr Southall. 'Shall we take a seat at the larger table?'

Lady Gayle followed her solicitor to the large oak table by the library windows and tried to concentrate as Mr Southall outlined all the terms of her father's will. There was a lot to focus on, and despite what she had said to her mother, she wasn't sure she was up to the task ahead.

When she bade Mr Southall farewell, all she wanted to do was lie down in her room, but she heard her mother calling for her as soon as her foot hit the carpeted tread of the first stair. *How on earth does she do that?* She changed tack and strolled to the drawing room.

Before she could lay her hand on the door handle, Fredericks slid from the shadows and opened the door. Lady Gayle jumped, glanced up at him, and he gave her a slight nod.

'Thank you,' she said. What else could she say? As children, she and Alfred had had to open doors for themselves. Even Maxwell, her cousin who had been heir to the estate, and his little brother Rupert opened their own doors. Under her breath, she muttered, 'I still don't think I am ever going to get used to this.'

The Dowager Countess reclined on one of the sofas with her toy dog, Lily. She was wafting herself with her handkerchief. 'What is to become of us?' she wailed. 'We cannot manage without a man to guide us.'

'Nothing is going to happen to us, Mama,' Lady Gayle replied. 'Your plans have not changed materially. Now I shall live here too. Everything will continue very much as it would have done should Papa not have died. I won't return to my life in London. The income from the estate will support us... at least to a certain extent—'

'How can you talk about money at a time like this? It's

extremely vulgar.' Lady Ethel pushed herself into a seated position and waved her crystal glass. Fredericks slid across the floor with a fresh gin, lemon and ice and took the offending glass away.

'We are going to need to talk about money a great deal more,' replied Lady Gayle. 'I shall spend some time with the land agent tomorrow, and the rest of the week I will be meeting the tenants, the farmers, and the shopkeepers. I shall perhaps pay a visit to the brewery.'

'A brewery! Why on earth would you visit a brewery?'

'It's *my* brewery, Mother. I shall visit it as often as I choose. Now, if you will excuse me, I need to lie down before dinner.' Lady Gayle swept from the room, the silk skirt of her dress managing a small, but satisfactory twirl. Nothing compared to the bustle of her mother's heavy, taffeta gowns, of course, and she wondered if she would have time, let alone the spare money, to travel to London for a whole new wardrobe. As she trudged up the stairs to her room, she reflected that any additions to her collection were more likely to consist of serviceable tweeds rather than flapper dresses.

Lady Gayle opened her bedroom door and sank onto the bed. It wasn't the room she'd used as a child when she, her brother, and her parents visited Lord Percival. That was on the next floor, near the nursery and consequently near the attics and servants' quarters. Briefly, she wondered if she should take over the room that her father had been using: the old Earl's room. She sighed deeply; *I am not ready for that yet.*

A rustle of starched garments made her realise she was not alone, and she cracked open one eye.

'Oh, it's you,' she said. 'Thank goodness.'

'Yes, just me,' replied Alice, her maid. 'Am I packing? When are we returning to London?'

Lady Gayle paused before answering. Alice loved the bustle of working in a London house and had expressed her displeasure at moving to the country. Although Bethencourt Castle was close to York, it was not the short cab ride to the music halls that Alice and the other maids were used to.

'We're...' Lady Gayle let out a long breath; this wasn't going to be easy. 'I'm so sorry, Alice. We're not going back to London. We'll be staying here. At least for the time being. I'm sorry. I know you're not fond of the countryside.'

Alice stopped pretending to tidy hairbrushes on the dressing table and whirled to face her mistress. 'What about the new earl?' she said.

'There isn't one. At least, it's not an earl,' replied Lady Gayle. 'You have the pleasure of addressing Countess Bethencourt. I am the new earl.'

Alice grasped the dressing table, her eyes wide and dark in her pale face. 'You can't be the earl,' she pronounced. 'You're not a man, and anyway, isn't the estate entailed away from the women in the family?'

Lady Gayle giggled. 'You are correct, Alice, and not correct. I can't be called Earl Bethencourt since, as you point out, I am not a man, but I have discovered, to my surprise, that the entailment ended with my father. He willed his estate to me, and so I have everything. The house, the title, the estate, and the fortune. Or at least what's left of it.' Lady Gayle dragged a pillow over her face and groaned.

'Not to mention all the responsibility,' said Alice.

Lady Gayle peeked out from under the pillow and sat,

swinging her feet to the floor. She covered her face with her hands as Alice removed her shoes. 'Just so. I feel as if I have aged twenty years simply thinking about the responsibility of running this place.

'Have you packed sufficient country clothes for a long stay? I'd only planned to be here long enough to see Mama and Papa settled.'

'I packed all the country clothes your ladyship possesses,' said Alice. 'Two tweed suits, one pair of stout shoes and one pair of boots. Your old riding habit was already here. It's been in mothballs, but it seems undamaged.'

'I haven't worn that since before the war. I won't be able to squeeze into it.'

'You may be surprised, milady. Especially since you've lost so much weight recently. In any case, there were some other riding habits in the attics which may suit.'

'You've been in the attics? I've not been up there since I was a child. You didn't meet the ghost, did you?'

Alice's lips narrowed so much they almost disappeared. 'I don't hold with ghosts, milady. Most unnatural. You don't get ghosts in London.'

Overcome by Alice's bravery, Lady Gayle suddenly felt very reticent. Despite her protestations to her mother, she was overwhelmed by what she was facing. 'You will be able to stay with me, won't you, Alice?' she said, holding out her hands to her maid. 'I should be terribly lost without you.'

Alice gave Lady Gayle's hands a quick squeeze. 'I shall stay as long as your ladyship needs me. We survived the war together, didn't we? I wouldn't desert you now. Now, are you going to need some more rest before dinner? Or are you rested enough? It's not a large party, is it?'

Lady Gayle gave Alice a faint smile. She reflected briefly on the time they had met, back when Lady Gayle had delivered patients to the hospital where Alice worked as a nursing assistant. Despite the bombs and bloodshed, driving an ambulance had been a lot easier than running a country estate was likely to be. She rubbed her eyes. 'No, it isn't. I'm glad you remembered we had guests. I'd completely forgotten,' she said. 'Fortunately, it's only Colonel and Mrs Gosforth. I do wish Mama had asked them to delay their visit for a few days though.'

'Yes, indeed, milady. I've laid out the beaded dress. Black as you're in mourning, but still rather stylish. I thought the black headband and a small ostrich feather?'

'Oh, Alice, what would I do without you?' She reclined on the bed and closed her eyes, brushing away a single tear as she recalled her time driving patients to the hospital on the Western Front and the very handsome and brave young man who was, so very briefly, her husband.

CHAPTER THREE

Lady Gayle gazed at herself in the mirror. The discreet ostrich feather in her headband certainly added a touch of glamour, but was it entirely appropriate on the evening of her father's funeral? She raised her hand to remove it as her mother burst into her bedroom.

'You can't possibly go down dressed like that,' gasped the Dowager Countess. 'Take that headband off at once.'

Lady Gayle stiffened and dropped her hands into her lap. She squeezed her hands together to stop them shaking. 'I shall not,' she replied. 'It's the fashion, and I should feel incomplete without it.'

'You should be in full mourning as I am. I will, of course, mourn your father's passing for a year, but I may follow the guidance of our dear queen and mourn him for the rest of my days.'

'Queen Victoria is dead, Mama,' Lady Gayle replied. 'She has been dead for over twenty years. Her grandson, King George, is on the throne now.' She took one last glance in the mirror. Alice had been right about the headband. It *was* perfect.

Following her mother out of the room, she took time to run her eye over her mother's garments. From a small white bonnet on top of her piled-up hair to the black bustle dress, she was a taller and slenderer replica of the late queen. It was not worth asking her mother to change her mode of dress and move with the times. She'd tried so often and failed and now, after Papa, what was the point? If Mama was happy being a Victorian relic, then who was she to argue?

More relics awaited her in the drawing room. Colonel and Mrs Gosforth were attired in the same Victorian style as her mother. Hair piled high on her head and wearing a long dress—Mrs Gosforth that was—not the colonel. The colonel had chosen a white tie and a frock coat instead of the more fashionable black tie and dinner jacket.

Lady Gayle greeted them both and took a sherry from the tray Fredericks offered.

'Dreadful business this, what?' blustered the colonel. 'First Percival and now your father. A bad run of luck, I'd say.'

'Peter,' hissed his wife behind her hand. 'It's not the time.'

'Nonsense,' her husband replied. 'What are you going to do, young lady? Sell up? Can't run it yourself, can you?'

Lady Gayle clenched her jaw. *How on earth does he know already?* She glanced at her mother, who refused to look her way. *Ah, that's how he knows.* 'Why can't I, Colonel?' she murmured, turning to the colonel, and giving him an angelic smile.

'Not a job for a woman, is it? Running an estate. Needs a man's logic. You'll have to find yourself a husband.'

'I see,' replied Lady Gayle. She looked over to where the

butler stood. He gave her a single nod of the head. She faced her guests. 'It would appear dinner is served.'

She waved away the colonel's arm. 'Thank you,' she said. 'Perhaps you could walk Mama into dinner. I think I can manage to find my own way. After all, that doesn't require too much logic.'

Colonel Gosforth glowered at her, but he offered his arm to Lady Ethel.

Biting back a laugh, Lady Gayle led her guests to the dining room. A large fire blazed in the grate, although the mirror above was still covered. It should have been taken down after the funeral and she decided to mention it to the housekeeper, Mrs Mitchell, after dinner.

As chief male guest, the colonel was placed to her right and Mrs Gosforth to her left. Mama was seated next to the colonel.

Fredericks, accompanied by a footman, brought in the soup course and the party fell silent as they consumed the watery liquid. At least there was no shortage of bread.

'This is the sort of thing I mean,' said Colonel Gosforth eventually. He pushed away his unfinished soup.

Lady Ethel gasped at the lapse in manners. Lady Gayle glanced over at her mother.

'What can you mean?' Lady Gayle said, allowing a simpering smile to play around her lips as she directed her gaze to the colonel. Her blue eyes shone hard and bright as sapphires.

'This soup. Not up to the standard we expected when your... what relation was Lord Percival to you exactly?'

'He was my father's first cousin—once removed, wasn't it, Mama? I always called him Great Uncle. However, Colonel Gosforth, I fail to understand the connection to the soup—'

'I was getting to that. When your great uncle,' he pronounced the last two words with heavy emphasis, 'was Earl Bethencourt, the fare was much better. A proper thick broth. None of this thin, watery stuff.'

'If I may, your ladyship.' Fredericks stepped away from hovering by the sideboard. His usual spot when dinner was being eaten.

'Please do,' replied Lady Gayle.

'Cook wanted to present you with something that would remind you of your recent travels in France, my lady. She thought this beef consommé would do just that.'

'It does indeed, Fredericks. Give my compliments to Mrs Wood. Her consommé is just perfect. Light on the stomach, bursting with flavour and beautifully clarified.'

'Thank you, my lady. I know she will be delighted.'

Lady Gayle nodded, and Fredericks resumed his post as guardian. 'Have you never had a consommé, Colonel Gosforth? I understood that you were in France during the Great War?'

'I was, but we ate our army rations. We rarely had time to go to restaurants. We were fighting a war, after all.'

'I'm not likely to forget.' Lady Gayle touched her fingertips to the thin gold band on her left hand, pausing for a moment as if in prayer. Then she shook her head, lifted her spoon, and continued with her soup.

After a few seconds, Colonel Gosforth pulled his bowl closer and finished his dish of consommé with every appearance of enjoyment.

The rest of the meal passed without comment, but at the end, the Dowager Countess rose. 'Oh,' she said and sat down again. 'I was going to suggest we leave the gentlemen to their cigars... perhaps you would like to come straight to the drawing room with the ladies tonight, Colonel?'

The colonel cleared his throat, a flush of colour rushing from his collar to his cheekbones. 'I wondered if Lady Gayle would stay for a moment. I have some private estate business I need to discuss, and since there is no male heir to discuss it with...'

'I understand. I'll have some coffee sent in. Fredericks?' The Dowager Countess strolled to the door where Fredericks was already holding it open for her and Mrs Gosforth.

Colonel Gosforth made his way to the sideboard and collected the decanter of port and two glasses.

Lady Gayle accepted the small glass of the sweet, heavy wine and took a tiny sip. 'Estate business?' she said. 'I buried my father today, and already you want to discuss something you must have previously discussed with him.'

The colonel dipped his head, clearing his throat again before gulping his entire glass of port. He instantly refilled his glass.

'There's a parcel of land by the river. Where it curves around the oak tree, I believe it belongs to my estate.'

'I see. And tell me, where did my father stand on this issue when you brought the matter to him?'

'He agreed to sign it over to me.'

Lady Gayle nodded and took another sip of her wine. 'Very interesting,' she said. 'Isn't that spot part of our trout stream?'

Colonel Gosforth finished his second glass of port. 'What of it?' He was on the point of pouring himself a third glass when Fredericks brought in a tray of coffee and biscuits.

The butler laid the tray on the end of the table with a slight bow. 'Will that be all, my lady?'

'No, not quite,' said Lady Gayle as she poured coffee into the delicate cups. 'Fredericks, would you happen to know where my father kept his maps of the Bethencourt Castle estate?'

'In his study or in the library, my lady. The library has a larger table for spreading maps about,' came the reply.

'Very well. Colonel, shall we adjourn to the library and Mr Fredericks, would you be so kind as to bring us the maps?' Lady Gayle strode from the room without waiting for the door to be opened. She knew the parcel of land in question, and it was highly unlikely that her father would have relinquished it easily. Not only was it the best trout fishing spot on the whole estate, but it had been a favourite place for her to spend time with her father and his cousin. Even as she thought of it, she imagined the river splashing over her short boots. When she learned to fish, her father ensured she had proper waders so that she could walk out into the river without getting wet feet. Cold feet were an entirely different matter, even with two pairs of woollen socks. Yet, despite the cold, it was a time that she had loved.

CHAPTER FOUR

When Fredericks entered the library, he spread the maps out on the large table where Lady Gayle had sat with her solicitor only hours before. With the help of two footmen, he arranged for the table to be moved into the centre of the room, and once he was satisfied with the arrangements, he placed another log on the fire. The colonel busied himself searching for the river and the parcel of land.

'There. That's it,' he shouted.

Fredericks silently wiped up the port that had been spilt on the map.

'Perhaps we should keep drinks away from the documents,' murmured Lady Gayle. 'These are my family history, after all.'

'What? Yes, dash it all.' The colonel placed his glass on the mantel and strode back to the table. 'There.' His pointing finger jabbed at a spot by the river.

Lady Gayle noticed the pencilled line around the parcel of land, which looked to be about two acres. There was a number jotted in one corner. 'Is that a reference number?' she asked, looking at Fredericks.

'Yes, my lady. You will find a corresponding number in the land ledger your great uncle kept. If the land changed hands at any time, there will be a record kept in there.'

'Thank you, Fredericks,' she said. 'Well, Colonel, it rather sounds like a task for when our heads are clearer.'

The colonel cleared his throat and dropped into an armchair by the now blazing fire. He poured more port, then offered the decanter to Lady Gayle.

Lady Gayle shook her head, having lost count of the number of glasses of fortified wine he'd consumed. She knew she wanted to remain sober for this conversation. 'Was there anything else you wanted to discuss, Colonel?'

He blinked at her, seemingly confused about where he was. 'I thought I could put you in touch with a good chap who can help you sell the place. Get you an excellent price, then you can go back to London and spend your time shopping and partying. All the things you young things like to do.'

Lady Gayle sat in the armchair opposite. Many of her London friends, weary of the bleak war years, were doing just that. A life of endless parties, drinking, drugs, and heaven alone knew what else. The Bright Young Things they'd been labelled, and although it was fun to spend a few days in their company, it was no longer a lifestyle she wanted for herself, even though her expectation had been that she would be returning to her London flat after her father's funeral. She was not the only one who was tired of the party life it seemed. Not two days ago, she'd received a letter from Lady Sylvia Redmond-Smythe begging for a few days in the country to recover from the constant partying and another one from Evelyn Trent, an old friend from her ambulance driving days. She decided to telegram Lady Sylvia in the morning and invite her to stay for a few days. Evelyn Trent, on the other hand, she would write to and put off for a few weeks. Her mother would be unable to bear too many house guests while she was in mourning.

Suddenly aware that the colonel was still speaking to her, Lady Gayle turned her gaze to him.

'I'm sorry, Colonel. My mind was elsewhere. What did you say?'

'That you need a man's brain to run this place. Women are too emotional and illogical. You ladies just don't have the mentality for serious work.'

'I did rather serious work during the war,' Lady Gayle reminded him.

Oblivious to the coolness of her tone, the colonel wittered on. 'But you were just in the yeomanry, weren't you?' he said, referring to the First Aid Nursing Yeomanry, an organisation which had placed nurses on the Western Front to tend to the wounded soldiers.

'I was a FANY,' she replied, using the name preferred by the FANYs in spite of or because of its slightly salacious tone. 'I was only eighteen, but I lied and said I was twenty. That made me old enough to drive ambulances, and since we were short of mechanics, in time, I learned how to repair engines. The sergeant said I was the best engineer he'd seen.'

'Well, yes, that's all very well. But I don't think it really changes things, does it—'

'It does, Colonel. It means that if I am capable of keeping an ambulance running, rescuing men from the front line, and saving their lives, then I am sure I have sufficient wits to run this estate.'

She rose and rang the bell; Fredericks was immediately by her side. 'Please, could you bring me my uncle's land ledger?' she said. 'It would appear the colonel, and I need to research a little something after all.'

Lady Gayle bit back a small smile. Was Fredericks' bow lower than usual? He returned promptly with the ledger and turned to the page containing the code of the parcel of land in question.

Lady Gayle ran her finger down the sheet and then flicked forward until the end of the page. 'There's only one entry,' she said. 'It seems my ancestor won that land and section of the river from your ancestor in 1813. See, it's listed here. Even the type of card game is mentioned. Vingt-et-un it would appear. There's no record of the land being won back.'

Colonel Gosforth slammed his glass onto the table beside him and marched to the map table. He snatched the ledger from Lady Gayle and began flicking through the pages.

She flushed but resisted the temptation to snatch the ledger back. 'Colonel, if you'd wanted to study the ledger yourself, you only had to ask.'

He glowered at her and continued his search. Eventually, when the information he sought didn't appear, he flung the ledger on the large table. 'You've not heard the last of this,' he roared as he flounced from the room.

Lady Gayle raised her glass to his retreating back and resumed her chair by the fire. She finished the glass of port and drank some of the cooling coffee. All the time she heard raised voices. The colonel, her mother, and more softly, Mrs Gosforth.

At last, all fell quiet, and she breathed a sigh of relief. About to join her mother in the drawing room, she heard the library door open.

'What on earth was all that about?' her mother said.

'The colonel was very upset. Gaspod snarled at him. You know that dog really shouldn't live in the house.'

'Only my illogical brain being logical. It appeared to annoy him dreadfully,' replied Lady Gayle. 'Fancy trout for dinner tomorrow, Mama? I think I might go out for a spot of fishing in the morning. I'll take Gaspod with me.'

After her mother had retired for the evening, Lady Gayle made her way to the kitchen to thank the staff—she couldn't yet think of them as *her* staff—for the lovely dinner they had prepared. As she entered the servants' hall, everyone leapt to their feet, and it took several minutes for her to convince them to be seated.

'I wanted to thank everyone,' she said. 'Not just for your help this evening but for everything that you've done since my father was taken ill.'

'It has been our pleasure, my lady,' replied Fredericks. His glance around the table was met with nods from all present. 'It is our deepest wish that you come to love the castle and the land as much as we do.'

'I'm very pleased to hear you say so,' said Lady Gayle. 'I have a lot to learn about running the estate and will need the help of all of you.'

This last comment was met with bowed heads and a few indistinct mumbles.

Lady Gayle caught the eye of Alice, who was nodding her head slightly in the direction of the stairs. Clearly, it was time to go. Realising she was beginning to outstay her welcome, Lady Gayle rose. All the staff followed suit, and she rushed from the room.

'Please make sure that doesn't happen again, Alice.' Lady Gayle heard Fredericks reprimand her maid. About to return upstairs, she hesitated on the bottom step but was unable to hear Alice's mumbled reply.

It was early morning when Lady Gayle awoke. She lit a candle—Uncle Percival had not seen fit to have electricity installed in all parts of the castle—and wandered to the window. She pulled aside the heavy curtains, but all seemed quiet in the formal gardens below her window. A vixen howled, and she jumped at the eerie sound. *Perhaps that's what woke me?* She strained her ears but heard no answering bark from the dog fox.

Pulling the curtains back over the window, she ambled towards her bed. Yawning, she sat on the edge of the bed and blew out the candle. For a moment, she sat in the dark, feeling the cold of the room envelope her. Out in the hallway, she heard a scuffling sound and lighting the candle once more; she ran to the door and looked out into the corridor. A figure scurried down the stairs, and she rushed to follow to see who it was. At the top of the stairs, she held up the candle. Nothing could be seen in its flickering light. Shivering, she decided it must either have been the ghost of Lord Robert Sheldrake, the first Earl of Bethencourt, or simply her imagination. She smiled, shaking her head at her nervousness as she returned to her bed. It was much more likely to have been one of the housemaids laying out the fires for the morning.

CHAPTER FIVE

WHEN SHE AWOKE THE SECOND TIME, THE MORNING DAWNED bright and clear, a perfect day to fish, but since she'd forgotten her appointment with the land agent, Lady Gayle's planned excursion had to be postponed.

Instead, the undergardener was dispatched by Mrs Woods, the cook, to procure trout for dinner. 'Go to the fishmonger if you can't catch any, but don't tell the mistress.'

He tapped his forefinger to his cap with a grin and set off. Fishing was a much better prospect than dead-heading roses.

Attired in an ancient riding habit, Lady Gayle made her way to the stables. As she passed the part of the yard given over to the care of the Bentley, she saw Chadwick polishing the car.

'Good morning, Chadwick,' she said.

The chauffeur took off his cap. 'Good morning, my lady. It's a fine day for a ride around the estate.'

'Indeed,' she said. 'Tell me, Chadwick, did you hear a car backfire yesterday? I thought perhaps the Bentley was running a bit rich, but when I came to look, you were just jumping in to start the engine.'

'The car is running extremely well, my lady,' replied Chadwick. Pink spots rose on his cheek. 'Would your ladyship like to hear the engine?'

Oh dear, I've offended him, thought Lady Gayle. 'No, I trust your judgement,' she said.

'Thank you, my lady,' replied Chadwick. 'Now you mention it, I did think I heard something yesterday afternoon. It could have been a car backfiring on the road, but I don't believe the sound would have been heard at the castle. It might have been a poacher in the woods.'

'I think you have heard as many guns being fired as I have, Chadwick. It wasn't a shotgun, was it?'

Chadwick scratched his head. 'No, my lady, I thought it sounded like a rifle. The colonel likes to take potshots at the rooks every so often.'

'Does he now?' she said. 'Is he a good shot?'

Chadwick dipped his head. 'I really couldn't say, my lady.' He nodded towards the stable yard. 'I think Mr Shepherd is waiting for you.'

Lady Gayle nodded and turning around, she saw Shepherd, the head groom, limping as he led Great Uncle Percival's grey gelding, Plantagenet, towards her. Shepherd also held the reins for a patient-looking bay mare.

Lady Gayle raised a gloved hand to stroke Plantagenet's forehead. The horse snickered and lowered his head for a scratch around the ears. Lady Gayle obliged, and the horse nuzzled her. Although she had noticed the side saddle in place, Shepherd still surprised her when he handed Plantagenet's reins to her. When her great uncle was alive, she was always made to ride Bessie.

'Plantagenet is far too strong for you, my dear,' Uncle Percival had constantly told her. Nothing had changed as far as Lady Gayle could see, except that Plantagenet now belonged to her and no one else.

Mr Shepherd cupped his hands to offer her a boost onto the horse's side saddle.

'I thought you'd prefer his lordship's horse, my lady. Mr Howden, the land agent, prefers Bessie. She's a nice, quiet ride for him. Between you and me,' Shepherd whispered, 'I think he's a bit scared of horses.'

'Who could be scared of Bessie?' Lady Gayle asked. Bessie had been given to her when she'd outgrown Sandy, the golden-coloured Shetland pony. How she sobbed when Sandy died. But that was long before the Great War, and there had been countless deaths since then. Naturally, with each additional death, there had been fewer tears.

Once seated on the gelding, Lady Gayle gathered the reins, resting her hands lightly on the pommel while she awaited the arrival of the land agent. Shepherd adjusted her stirrup leathers and tightened the girth.

'Where can he have got to, Shepherd?' she said. 'I don't have all day to wait upon his pleasure.'

'I can send the boy to the house, my lady. But he does normally drive to the stables.'

As Shepherd spoke, the rumble of a car engine was heard, and the Austin 7 shuddered to a stop close by the tack room. Lady Gayle shuddered in sympathy. Its plugs needed attention. She'd mention it on their ride around the estate.

Mr Howden unfolded himself from the car, placed his

hat on his head and perched his thick glasses on the end of his nose.

Lady Gayle surmised that he must be over six feet tall. *He's going to look ridiculous on Bessie. His feet will virtually touch the ground.*

'Countess Bethencourt,' said the newcomer, raising his hat and bowing slightly. 'I'm Harold Howden, the land agent. May I say how sorry I am for your loss?'

'Thank you,' replied Lady Gayle. 'But you needn't be quite so formal. Lady Gayle will be fine.' She noticed a flicker of amusement curve his lips. Gold flecks in his hazel eyes flashed before he regained control of his face. *Oh dear, is he mocking me? Maybe Alice was right, and he really is a Bolshie.* She knew Alice liked to amuse her with the rumours she heard.

The Bolsheviks, a Russian political group, had overseen the demise of the Romanovs, the last Russian royal family. It had been a bloodbath, and fear spread throughout Europe that other aristocratic families would meet the same fate. Although they had not encountered a similar demise, the fear remained all the same. It had not diminished in the five years since the killings.

Lady Gayle resisted the urge to scratch her head. What was it about this man that was making her glow like this? *I do hope he's not a Bolshie; he's far too handsome.*

Mr Howden took Bessie's reins from Shepherd and accepted a boost onto the saddle. The bay cob bore his weight valiantly, but as Lady Gayle had surmised, Mr Howden's legs were far too long and hung below the mare's stomach.

'Shepherd, don't we have another horse for Mr Howden? Surely old Seamus would be a better fit?'

'He would that, my lady, but—'

'Please don't trouble on my account,' said the land agent. 'Bessie and I have become used to each other.'

'That's as may be, Mr Howden, but you look ridiculous. Bessie is far too small for you, and you are too heavy for her. Shepherd, saddle up Seamus, will you?'

Mr Shepherd strode over to the loose boxes, calling for one of the stable lads to assist. Within moments, he returned with a large Welsh cob, dray horse mix.

Lady Gayle nodded and turned to smile at Mr Howden. If she was startled by his ashen face, she chose not to mention it.

Silently, Mr Howden climbed onto the mounting block and allowed himself to be boosted onto Seamus. It was hard to ignore his widened eyes as he looked down at the ground from his new elevation.

'Very good,' said Lady Gayle. 'Shall we go? You can lead the way, Mr Howden.'

He gave her a thin-lipped nod and tried to encourage Seamus to walk ahead of Plantagenet, but Seamus planted his giant hooves and shook his head.

'This is why we shouldn't be using horses any longer,' said Mr Howden. 'They simply cannot be trusted. It makes much more sense to use motor cars. Everywhere on the estate is now accessible by car. If I had my way, every horse on the estate would be shot and sold for dog meat. Think of the money you would save.'

'Thank you for your advice, Mr Howden,' replied Lady Gayle coldly. She didn't dare look at the head groom, knowing he would be as upset as she was. 'However, I happen to like horses around the place and plan to keep them as long as possible. Now, perhaps I should take the lead if you can't persuade Seamus. Where are we going first?'

'Mr Winterbottom at Hall Farm. Do you know the way?' he snapped.

Lady Gayle raised a single blonde eyebrow at the land agent. *Perhaps he's not so handsome after all.* Ignoring Mr Howden's tone, she nodded her thanks to the head groom and set off at a smart trot, paying no attention to whether Mr Howden could keep up or not.

The path to Hall Farm, which the Winterbottom family tenanted, narrowed through the woods. The trees drew together overhead, creating a dark tunnel. To the right, at the base of a severely steep slope, water rushed along in a fast-running brook. Lady Gayle drew Plantagenet to a halt and twisted in the saddle to see what had happened to the land agent. After a few moments, Seamus plodded into view with the hapless Mr Howden, who stared down the slope at the racing water.

'Don't look down, Mr Howden,' Lady Gayle called to him.

He gave her a tight-lipped grimace; it could hardly be described as a smile. Although, after their contretemps, a smile would have been somewhat surprising. Horse and rider continued their lazy plod.

Lady Gayle groaned. *Do I have to take him with me to meet all the tenants? It will take forever unless he can smarten up his pace.* 'I'll show this horse-murdering Bolshie,' she muttered to herself.

As the riders neared Hall Farm, a five-bar gate closed off the lane. Lady Gayle glanced at Mr Howden, who was still plodding along several paces behind her. With a quick grin, she gathered her horse into a canter and readied him for the jump. Plantagenet sailed over the gate, landing perfectly on the other side. Behind her, Lady Gayle heard the shouts of the land agent. Seamus trotted rapidly to the gate where, head down, he stopped. Mr Howden didn't, and he sailed over the gate. His landing was far from perfect.

'You absolute blithering idiot,' shouted Mr Howden as he turned to face Lady Gayle. 'You could have killed me.' He clambered to his feet, using the gate for support as he dusted himself down and checked for damage to his clothes.

Lady Gayle glanced down at him. Whilst she rarely put on airs and graces, she was not used to being called a "blithering idiot" by anyone. Walking her horse to the gate, she leaned down and opened it, collected Seamus, walked both horses through to the other side and leaned down to close the gate again. She threw Seamus's reins to Mr Howden. 'I'll meet you in the farmyard,' she said coldly.

CHAPTER
SIX

Touching her heels to Plantagenet's side, Lady Gayle trotted down the hill towards the whitewashed farmhouse. Chickens scattered as horse and rider wandered into the courtyard. Lady Gayle released her leg from the side saddle and slipped to the ground. She tethered Plantagenet to a rail where he could drink from the cattle trough. Then she eased out the kinks in her shoulders as she looked around. After a moment, a woman with dark, straggly hair rushed out of the house.

'We weren't expecting you on your own, your ladyship,' she said. 'Where is Mr Howden? Will you take tea?'

'Mr Howden fell off his horse,' Lady Gayle replied with a grin. 'He'll be here in a moment, and yes, I'd love a cup of tea. Do you still make those ginger biscuits you made when I was a girl?'

'I do indeed, milady.' Mrs Winterbottom bobbed into something that resembled a half curtsy. 'I'm surprised you remember, but I baked some just in case.'

'They were the highlight of all my farm visits,' replied Lady Gayle. She checked her horse once more, easing his girth so he could drink his fill. Her horse attended to; she followed Mrs Winterbottom into the kitchen. Standing in the doorway and blinking while her eyes became used to the dim light, she eventually crossed over the threshold before looking around. Nothing had changed since she was a child visiting with Lord Percival. The same warmth from the oven, the same delicious smells of hot bread and scones. The tin of biscuits was brought over, and as Lady Gayle bit into one, the rich, buttery taste melted on her tongue. Years floated away, and she was a child once more. Sandy was waiting for her in the yard, and her father was still alive. Tears pricked at her eyes, and she brushed them away, annoyed, and embarrassed.

Turning her head as hooves clattered in the yard, Lady Gayle watched Mrs Winterbottom run to the door, calling for her husband. Mr Howden strode into the house.

'That was stupid and irresponsible,' he said, his hands on his hips. 'You could have been killed. Your horse could have tripped in a rabbit hole. Anything could have happened, and I would have been blamed for everything. Even if your impetuosity wasn't my fault.'

Lady Gayle glanced in his direction. 'I've been riding since before I could walk, Mr Howden,' she said. 'I'm also quite capable of galloping and checking for rabbit warrens at the same time. In any case, it's unlikely there would be any in the middle of a farm track.

'Furthermore, Mr Howden, I'm not used to being called names, and I'd be grateful if you didn't repeat your behaviour of today.' Lady Gayle folded her arms, noticing that at least the land agent had the grace to look embarrassed.

'I am sorry, your ladyship,' he said, head bowed. 'But—'

'I don't think I need your help introducing me to my

tenants,' she said. 'As you can see, I've known most of them since I was a child.' With that, she shook hands with Mr Winterbottom, ignoring his mud-covered hands and followed him into the farmyard, chatting away as if she'd been the landlord for years.

Lady Gayle left the land agent to nurse his bruises with Mrs Winterbottom and to make his own way back to the stables at Bethencourt Castle. Alone, she carried on the task of meeting her tenants and listening to their problems. She made a mental note to speak to her solicitor about replacing the obnoxious land agent. However handsome he was, she decided he was a Bolshie after all. She blushed at the insults he'd thrown at her, although she had been called worse by the sergeant when she was a trainee mechanic. But that wasn't the point, she told herself.

When she returned to the stables with Plantagenet, walking him the last mile so that he wasn't sweaty and damp when he went into his stable, Mr Howden had already departed. A pool of oil marked the place where he'd left his car. *So much for being more efficient than horses. Cars are only any good if you take care of them.*

She strolled into the yard, and young Billy came to take Plantagenet from her. The stable lad was hardly tall enough to reach the horse's withers, yet the grey followed him meekly. Lady Gayle found a bucket of sand; several sat around the yard in case of fire and poured some over the patch of oil. At least now, it wouldn't spread.

Mr Shepherd appeared as she was replacing the bucket. 'You could have told me to do that, your ladyship,' he said, taking the bucket from her hand. He refilled it from an old, dilapidated trough that sat in one corner of the yard.

'It was fine, but I've just covered the oil. It will need sweeping up when the sand has soaked up the worst of it.' She regarded her handiwork for a moment. 'Did Mr Howden get back safely?'

Shepherd dipped his head, but she could see from the corner of his mouth, the grin which had spread across his face.

'Mr Howden was a little upset, your ladyship. I've given Seamus a hot mash for his supper, a reward for getting Mr Howden back in one piece.'

'I'm sure he appreciates it.'

'Mr Howden or Seamus, my lady?'

Lady Gayle chuckled but said nothing.

When Lady Gayle returned to her bedroom, Alice was filling the bath with hot water. The steamy room smelled delicious.

'I thought you'd need a nice soak after a long day out,' Alice said. 'Lady Redmond-Smythe arrived earlier. She's lying down before dinner.'

'Thank you, Alice. I wasn't expecting her for a couple of days,' replied Lady Gayle. 'How on earth did she get here so quickly?'

'Her maid said they'd been with Lord and Lady Ridgewell at St Nesbans House.'

'Oh, I see, well that's not far away at all. Jolly good job she got the telegram. Listen, I'm absolutely starving. I don't think I can wait until dinner.' Lady Gayle stood whilst Alice unbuttoned the riding habit. Once divested of most of her clothing, she stepped into the bath, removing her camisole and knickers once hidden by the water. She slid down until her head was covered and scratched at her head. It was itching after being under her riding hat all day.

'I asked Cook to prepare you a tray. I thought you'd be hungry. Shall I call for it now?'

'Oh, that would be divine. Thank you, Alice.'

Alice crossed the room to ring the bell while Lady Gayle sat in her bath, lathering the soap to wash her aching body. It was always the same when she came into the country—getting used to riding. It used so many muscles one didn't use when strolling in the parks of London.

When Alice returned, she washed her ladyship's hair and then helped her from the bath. The maid combed her mistress's hair while the latter ate ravenously.

'Careful,' Alice said. 'Or you won't get into your evening dress.'

Lady Gayle glanced at Alice for a moment and then returned her attention to her food. Once replete, she sat in front of the fire to dry her hair. She loved the new shorter styles, which dried so much quicker than the long hair she had endured during the war years.

She rested on her bed, dozing lightly until the dinner gong rang. She had just enough time to dress before the second gong, and her eagerness to see Sylvia again ensured she was ready in a trice. She skipped downstairs, all the aches from the day's riding forgotten.

CHAPTER SEVEN

THE DRAWING ROOM WAS EMPTY WHEN SHE WENT IN. GASPOD, the bloodhound, and Molly, the springer spaniel, had secured their normal positions by the fire but thumped their tails on the hearth rug at seeing her. She poured herself a small gin, joined the dogs by the fire and waited.

'Lady Sylvia Redmond-Smythe,' Fredericks intoned.

Sylvia swept into the room, a perfect vision in a white beaded frock which finished just below the knee. Like Sylvia, the garment was very daring. Her fair hair was bobbed and finger-curled whilst the sides were held back by diamond clips which glinted in the firelight. She held a cigarette holder with an unlit cigarette. This she wafted in the general direction of the fire, but it only lit once Fredericks held a match for her.

Once the charade with the cigarette was complete, the women hugged. Lady Gayle recalled how much she hated the smell of cigarettes, although the one Sylvia was smoking smelt different. Turkish perhaps? It had a woody, slightly spicy aroma.

'How absolutely lovely to see you, darling Gigi,' Sylvia

squealed, using the nickname that Lady Gayle only heard from her more flamboyant friends. Lady Sylvia's voice had always been high pitched and inclined to grate after a few days of sharing a house.

'How are Binky and Bundle?' said Lady Gayle. Lord Ridgewell, or Binky as he was known to his closest friends, was married to Barbara Newell. The Honourable Barbara Newell had attended the same girls' school as Gayle and Sylvia. Lady Gayle had lost touch with Barbara since her wedding the year before.

'Absolutely wonderful, darling. Devastatingly divine house. Bundle is expecting a bundle too. But all the same, she always puts on a terrific party.

'But I need a rest, darling. Some of your countryside peace and quiet. It must be wonderful to sit around with nothing to do day after day.'

Lady Gayle raised her eyebrows. She looked down at her reddened hands, thinking that she must get Alice to find the riding gloves that went with the habit she'd worn that morning. She had toyed with the idea of riding breeches but wasn't sure if North Yorkshire was ready for women in trousers. All morning, she'd heard tell of the women's land army and their breeches. Even after six years, the shock amongst her tenants was still palpable.

'I've been keeping myself busy,' Lady Gayle replied. 'I thought we could go for a ride tomorrow, and I can show you the estate.'

'Is it absolutely huge, darling? You'll have queues of young men wanting to be your next husband.'

'I don't want another husband.' Lady Gayle dipped her head. She took a drink from the tray that Fredericks offered. 'I had one, and even if there were any young men left, I'm happy on my own.'

'Oh yes, of course, Gigi. If you say so.' Sylvia sucked on her cigarette and blew a cloud of smoke to the ceiling. 'I suppose I should tell you; I'm heading down the aisle soon. Charles Vickery made me an offer, and I decided to accept him this time.'

'Congratulations.' Lady Gayle held up her glass. 'Perhaps we should have some champagne instead?'

'You're not upset, are you, Gigi? I know Felicity Makepeace, the racing driver, is furious, and of course, Charles was one of your beaus before the war.' Lady Sylvia tilted her head to one side whilst blowing out more smoke.

'No, I'm not in the least bit upset. Of course, I'm not. He never asked me to marry him, and we were far too young in any case.' Lady Gayle took another sip of her sherry. *I mustn't get tipsy.* 'So how about that ride in the morning?'

'I didn't bring any riding togs. Can you lend me some?' Lady Sylvia replied.

Lady Gayle nodded. 'Yes, my maid has found heaps of clothes in the loft. She can show your maid, and we'll kit you out in the morning.'

'Oh, don't speak to me about that girl. She's useless, I tell you. Utterly useless.'

'Your maid?' said Lady Gayle, 'Oh dear, I am sorry to hear that. Where did you find her?'

'She came from an agency, I believe. I would tell her to leave, but it's so dashed difficult to find staff these days, isn't it?'

Lady Gayle dipped her head as warmth flooded her face. Her own staff were excellent, inherited as they were from her great uncle. She could only hope that they would stay as it was unlikely that she would be able to offer wages to match what was to be had by the jobs on offer in the towns.

Lady Sylvia stubbed out her cigarette and threw the butt-end into the fire. Rifling in her beaded handbag, she brought out a small canister and a minuscule spoon, which she filled with white powder, and oblivious to the impact she was having, she continued with her administration of the drug.

Horrified at her guest's blasé behaviour, Lady Gayle could only look on speechless. However, she found her voice when offered the cocaine herself.

'No, thank you,' she replied. 'I don't anymore.' Her increasing dependence on the drug was one of the reasons she'd run away from London and agreed to help her parents settle into Bethencourt Castle. Once the war was over and she was unable to hide away with busy work, there was no choice but to face the grief of losing her husband. She snatched a breath, blinking away tears caused by the memory of that time and the physical pain of her grief. *No, I won't take that poison again.*

When Fredericks entered to say that dinner was served, Lady Gayle ushered her guest into the dining room with a haste that bordered on unseemly.

Fredericks had placed them together at one end of the long table as per Lady Gayle's request. Her mama had decided to take a tray in her room this evening. The Dowager Countess said she found Lady Sylvia's tone a little too shrill at times.

Dinner and conversation afterwards passed uneventfully. Lady Gayle found her gaze drifting to the beaded clutch bag, only too aware of the drug that was hidden inside.

. . .

The ladies exchanged news of mutual acquaintances, but at eleven o'clock, even Lady Sylvia was flagging.

'You must excuse me,' she said. 'It's been a very long day travelling. What time for our ride?'

'How about eleven o'clock? That will give you a chance to have a lie-in and a later breakfast,' said Lady Gayle.

Lady Sylvia kissed her on the cheek, and both ladies retired for the night.

After breakfast and attired in matching riding habits, Ladies Gayle and Sylvia wandered to the stables. After a delivery of roses arrived from London, they each attached a delicious pink rose to their left lapels.

'Like twins,' Lady Sylvia giggled as they surveyed themselves in the mirror.

Mr Shepherd had Plantagenet and Bessie saddled and readied. However, as soon as Lady Gayle was ready to mount, a footman from the house hurried over.

'I'm sorry, your ladyship. The Dowager Countess wants you back at the house.'

'Can't it wait?' her ladyship snapped.

Owens reddened. 'I was told to make sure you came back, my lady. Sorry, my lady.'

'Very well,' she replied. She threw Plantagenet's reins at Lady Sylvia. 'He was my uncle's horse. I've taken him out a few times, but he still has plenty of energy. I think you'll enjoy the challenge. Just remember to keep the river on your left. If you do that, you'll stay on Bethencourt land, and you should find your way back easily enough.'

Lady Sylvia arched her eyebrows at her friend. 'Very well,' she said. 'But if I get lost forever, you're going to have to explain to Charles why you let me go alone.'

'Plantagenet will take care of you.' Lady Gayle patted the horse on his neck. 'If worst comes to worst, he'll come home when he's hungry.'

Lady Gayle marched to the house to see what her mother wanted.

The Dowager Countess, however, denied all knowledge of the summons. 'Now that you are here, you can tell me how long that young woman will be staying?'

'Lady Sylvia is my guest, Mama. She'll be here for a few more days, and then she'll go back to London.'

'Will you be returning with her?'

'How can I, Mama? I have responsibilities here now. I can't just abandon my work here.'

'You could look for another husband,' replied her mother.

Lady Gayle removed her riding gloves one finger at a time while she attempted to regain her composure. She laid the gloves on a large oak sideboard and took a seat opposite her mother. 'I'd prefer not to discuss this topic any further, Mama, but since you've brought it up again, there will be no searches for a replacement for Hugh,' she said, running her hand over her stomach, her eyes misting at the memories.

She'd met Viscount Hugh Sexton when he was injured and transported him in her ambulance to the field hospital. He was unlike the other young men she'd met before: grave and sensitive but with a humorous side that made her giggle like a girl. One afternoon, although she knew she should not have been on the ward, she sat by his bed, reading the locally produced newspaper to him. He chuckled, although he was in pain from the bullet wound. When she raised her hand to stroke his sunken cheek and traced her fingers over his lips, he turned his head and pressed those lips into the hollow of her hand. A thrill of electricity shot through her, and she squealed out loud. A noise that only brought down upon her the attention of the ward sister—Sister Edwards—a solid Welshwoman in her late fifties who stood no nonsense on her ward.

'But a new husband doesn't have to be a replacement. You don't have to marry for love,' said her mother.

Biting back her emotions and unable to continue the conversation any longer, Lady Gayle simply replied, 'Mama, we will not discuss this again. Now, if you'll excuse me, I have work to do.' She retired to the library to enjoy a cup of tea, study the papers that the land agent had left for her, and hope that Sylvia was having a good time.

The remainder of the morning passed quietly. After luncheon, Lady Gayle took the time to write to her friend Evelyn Trent to suggest a visit in two weeks' time, at the beginning of December. Afterwards, she dealt with papers sent by her solicitor and then, whilst sitting at a silent afternoon tea with her mother, Fredericks came into the drawing room. 'I am very sorry to interrupt, my lady, there's disturbing news from the stables. Plantagenet has returned without his rider. Mr Shepherd has organised a search party, but she's nowhere to be found.'

'Oh lor,' said Lady Gayle. 'I thought she must be back and was resting. I had hoped she'd be able to manage him. Is the horse lame?'

'No, my lady, the horse appears to be in perfect health, apart from some blood drops on his shoulder. They're not his. Mr Shepherd has checked.'

Lady Gayle blanched and rose. 'We need to find her,' she said. 'Ask Shepherd to saddle Seamus for me. Can someone fetch Gaspod? It's time he earned his keep.'

Fredericks blinked.

'Yes, I know my mother has had the poor dog relegated to the stables. Tell Mr Shepherd to ready the dog. And get Alice to bring something from Lady Sylvia's room for Gaspod to get her scent.'

CHAPTER EIGHT

Lady Gayle rushed to the stables and checked her uncle's horse before anything else. As Mr Shepherd had said, there were no cuts on the animal, so the blood could not be his.

When Alice arrived with Lady Sylvia's beaded dress, Gaspod was presented with the all-important scent. He howled and strained at his leash.

'Alice, can you telephone the doctor and bring him to the stables when he arrives? I'll try to send someone back to the house with a message to tell you where we are as soon as we find her.'

'Yes, milady,' she said before sprinting back to the house.

'Let's go,' announced Lady Gayle. She mounted Seamus and followed Mr Shepherd, the dog, and the other stable lads out of the yard. Darkness was falling, but the lads all carried lanterns to light their way.

Ahead, Mr Shepherd wheezed and panted as he tried to keep pace with the straining hound. Of course, it would make some sense to release the hound and let him find Lady Sylvia, but they would then have the problem of keeping up with or finding the dog. Lady Gayle was grateful that she at least was able to ride.

They followed the path that she had taken the day before with the land agent. Nothing seemed amiss; the path was clear. Nothing for horse or rider to trip upon. She rode carefully, knowing that they were approaching the steep slope of the bank.

Lanterns swayed in front of her, blinding her momentarily.

Gaspod was still pulling on his leash when Mr Shepherd called for a lantern. He raised it high above his head and gasped.

Lady Gayle slid from her horse and ran to his side. She peered down the slope, but the light was too faint to see anything.

'She must be down there, my lady,' puffed Mr Shepherd. 'Gaspod knows.'

'Very well. Did we bring ropes?'

'Here, milady.' Billy held up a coil of rope. 'I'll tie it to the tree and take a look.' The boy wrapped one end of the rope around the tree and the other around his waist. The other two lads created a loop to ease him down the slope.

Lady Gayle stroked Seamus's neck whilst she waited, but she didn't have to wait long.

Billy called up. 'She's here. I think she's dead.'

'Impossible,' her ladyship shouted. Sylvia was far too full of life. She couldn't be dead. She was getting married, for heaven's sake. Lady Gayle dropped the horse's reins and rushed closer to the edge of the slope. 'I'm coming down,' she said.

Mr Shepherd placed a hand on her arm. 'That's not a good idea, my lady. We don't want you to slip too.'

'Is that what you think happened? That she simply

slipped? Why would there be blood on Plantagenet if she'd fallen and slipped? That doesn't make any sense,' she replied.

'You,' she said, pointing to one of the other boys. 'Take Seamus and let Alice and Dr Sloane know where we are.'

The boy only hesitated a second before leaping onto the old Welsh cob and trotting off down the path.

Billy clambered back up the slope, hanging on to the rope with one hand and clods of earth with the other. He collapsed on the path and hung his head between his knees.

Lady Gayle dropped to the ground and untied the rope, placing it around her own waist. 'I have to check,' she said. 'Give me a lantern and lower me down.'

'It's not safe, my lady,' said Mr Shepherd.

'I'm going down there. With your help or without it,' she retorted.

With a single nod, Shepherd took up a bight of the rope, and Lady Gayle eased herself over the edge, wishing she'd put on breeches instead of her tweed skirt. It was impossible to move down the slope with the lantern, so she left it on the path. 'Lower the lantern to me when I'm down there,' she said. She saw Shepherd's eyes widen, but he nodded when she raised her eyebrows at him.

She climbed down into the darkness with chattering teeth. Goosebumps rose on her arms and legs as she neared the brook.

When she reached Sylvia, she untied the rope, and while she waited for the lantern, she fumbled around to see if she could find a pulse in Sylvia's wrist. There was nothing, but she kept probing in case she wasn't feeling in the correct place. It was only something she'd seen the nurses do on the wards.

When the lantern dropped next to her, she used its light to check over Lady Sylvia's body. There was a gash on Sylvia's head where she'd hit it on a rock. *But the rock is down here; where did the blood on the horse come from?* Peering closer, she soon found the cause. By Lady Sylvia's left shoulder, there was a small hole in the fabric of the riding habit. Lady Gayle touched it with her fingertips. *What's that stickiness?* She inspected her fingertips under the lamp light. Blood. The idleness of her post-war years fell away, and she hunched her shoulders, almost expecting to hear shells bursting around her. She put the lantern down but could not find a place for it to sit without falling into the water, so she gave up on the idea of trying to roll her friend's body over. Instead, she reached underneath Lady Sylvia's shoulder as far as she could. Probing around with her fingers in a very businesslike manner, she hunted until she found what she was looking for—an exit wound. The stickiness was more plentiful here, and she pulled her hand away, wiping the thick blood onto the grass. During her time as an ambulance driver and mechanic during the Great War, she'd seen enough for her to know a gunshot injury when she saw one.

Refusing to ascend and leave her friend alone, Lady Gayle sat shivering by the rushing stream. When she heard raised voices above her, she rose but collapsed to the damp ground again. Her legs had seized and were unable to hold her weight.

'Lady Gayle,' came a voice she recognised as that of Dr Sloane. 'I need you to come up before I can get down there to my patient.'

'She's dead, doctor,' Lady Gayle called back.

'I'm very sorry,' he replied. 'I still need to be down there. We won't be able to get her back to the castle without a stretcher.'

Lady Gayle wrapped the rope around her waist once more and scrambled up the slope. The lantern she left lying below nestled against Sylvia's body.

Once back on the path, she was pleased to see her maid Alice had a warm coat ready for her.

'Cook made up a flask of soup for you, milady. I've brought you some dry stockings and shoes.'

Lady Gayle looked around at the men surrounding them both. 'I think just the coat and the soup, Alice,' she said. 'Thank you for showing the doctor the way.'

Alice nodded. 'We'll hide behind a tree, and you will put some dry clothes on,' replied Alice firmly. 'Otherwise, you'll catch your death of cold, and I don't want to explain to the Dowager Countess why I let that happen.'

Lady Gayle grinned. 'Very well,' she said. 'Soup first, though.' Nothing was going to induce her to change in public, even if she was hiding behind an oak tree.

Alice poured the hot soup into a cup and passed it to her mistress. As Lady Gayle drank, Alice unpacked sandwiches and placed them on a china plate.

Sitting on a log in the dark, eating sandwiches and soup from chinaware whilst waiting for her friend's body to be recovered from a muddy bank, felt very incongruous to Lady Gayle. She wanted to smile at the absurdity of it all, but all mirth subsided as she heard the calls from the men. She sat listening to the creak of the ropes as men and tree took the strain. Finally, Lady Sylvia's remains arrived on the bridleway.

Dr Sloane scrambled over the edge, taking a moment to

right himself. He oversaw Lady Sylvia onto the stretcher, and two of the grooms carried the stretcher away.

'I think you should get back to the castle, Lady Gayle,' said Dr Sloane. 'I need to ensure that you are not suffering unduly from your recent encounter.'

'Yes, doctor,' said Alice. 'We'll be going back to the castle directly.' To her mistress, she said. 'Are you able to ride milady?'

Lady Gayle nodded mutely and allowed herself to be hoisted back onto Seamus's side saddle. The old boy was certainly earning his hot mash this week. She grasped the reins and eased the horse around on the narrow path. Then she followed the silent stretcher bearers back to Bethencourt Castle.

CHAPTER NINE

The castle was in uproar when she returned. Supported by Alice and Fredericks, Lady Gayle made it to her room, where, at last, she was able to change into dry clothes in private. Although she was no prude, her experiences as a mechanic attached to the FANY organisation had left her with scant regard for men; thus, she preferred to disrobe in private, maintaining her modesty and her dignity.

Scarcely had she fastened her blouse when her mother rushed into the room.

'What on earth has been going on?' cried the Dowager Countess.

Lady Gayle blinked in surprise. Her mother never showed emotion. It was another way in which she followed the example of the late queen.

'Lady Sylvia has been killed,' Lady Gayle replied, dropping into a chair by the fire. The simple words had a devastating effect on her mother.

The Dowager Countess staggered to an armchair and collapsed in it. On the other side of the hearth, Lady Gayle held her hands towards the warmth of the fire.

Lady Ethel clutched her hand to her bosom. 'Killed? Are you sure?'

'Yes, I'm sure, Mama. I sat with her while we waited for Dr Sloane. Her body was quite cold.'

'I see,' replied her mother. To Alice, she said, 'I think I may take a small pick-me-up.'

Alice dipped a curtsy and hurried out of the room. After a short while, she returned with Fredericks weighed down by a tray of glasses. Behind the butler, dressed today in his footman's uniform, was her father's valet, Owens, with a loaded drinks trolley. Fredericks poured a gin for the Dowager Countess, nodded to the footman, and they departed.

Lady Ethel sank the contents in one gulp and held out her glass to Alice for a refill. 'There was a policeman downstairs. He wanted to talk to you, but I told him that was impossible. I said he could speak to you in the morning. He became quite insistent, and so I had Fredericks escort him from the premises.'

Lady Gayle had a quick grin at the thought of the local constable being ejected forcibly from Bethencourt Castle. He was a kindly man who had never punished her for her childhood pranks. Her mother's next question quelled her smile.

'Are you going to continue bringing disgrace upon the family name?'

Lady Gayle gave her mother a sharp glance. 'Disgrace?' she said. 'Alice, I think I need a pick-me-up too.' Alice lifted the brandy decanter from the drinks trolley. Lady Gayle accepted a glass from her maid with a nod. 'That will be all for now.'

Alice rushed from the room, closing the door quietly behind her.

'I think you had better explain yourself, Mother,' Lady Gayle sighed. 'How have I brought disgrace to the family?'

'You wanted to avoid being presented at Court. You ran away to join the Women's Yeomanry, and then you married a soldier. If that's not disgrace, then I am sure I do not know what is.'

'Mother, becoming a debutante when we were facing a war seemed extremely silly. I wanted to be useful rather than sit at home twiddling my thumbs. As for my soldier—' Lady Gayle spat the last word. 'My soldier was a viscount. Exactly the kind of man you wanted me to hunt down and marry. Before the war changed everything, look around you, Mother. The world is changing.'

'It's not changing for the better,' sniffed her mother. 'All these short dresses and women smoking. Votes for women and these dreadful Bright Young Things. It's an absolute travesty.'

'It's the modern world, Mother—the twentieth century. Despite what you think, the world is changing for the better. Or at least it was.'

She raised her head at a knock at her bedroom door.

'Come in,' she said.

The door opened a crack, and Dr Sloane peeked around the edge. 'How are you feeling?'

'She's fine, doctor. Nothing wrong with her at all,' the Dowager Countess announced. She pulled her dressing gown close. 'You can go. We'll call you if we need you again.'

Lady Gayle rose from her chair and glowered at her mother. 'Thank you, Dr Sloane,' she said, opening the door to admit the doctor. 'I *am* quite well. Do you know what killed Lady Sylvia?'

Lady Ethel rose. 'This is exactly what I'm talking about,'

she said. 'How could you invite someone to stay who was going to get themselves killed?'

'I hardly think it was what Lady Sylvia had planned when she asked to visit,' replied Lady Gayle. 'Good morning, Mother.'

The Dowager Countess swept from the room, her silk dressing gown billowing behind her.

Lady Gayle breathed a sigh of relief, nodding her thanks to Alice, who returned to chaperone her. 'Please sit down, doctor,' she said, indicating the chair her mother had just vacated.

Dr Sloane placed his medical bag on the floor and took the chair. 'What do *you* think happened?'

'Me? How should I know? I wasn't there. We were going to go riding together. Mother called me back to the house, and Lady Sylvia went alone. She took Uncle Percival's horse, Plantagenet. Although,' Lady Gayle sighed, 'I suppose he's my horse now.'

'Indeed,' replied the doctor. 'Lady Sylvia was shot with a rifle. A straight through and through wound from her shoulder and exiting from her upper back. A very good shot, if I may say so, but it wasn't only that which killed her. She hit her head when she fell and then bled out from the gunshot. If she had not been knocked unconscious, she may have been able to call for help.'

'I see.' Lady Gayle strolled back towards the fire. 'Who do we know locally who is good enough to make such a shot?'

'I think that would be a matter for the police, don't you?' replied Dr Sloane. 'I think it might be too complex for the local bobby, although I did let him know what happened. I've taken the liberty of sending a telegram to

Scotland Yard. You should expect a detective tomorrow or the day afterwards at the latest.'

Lady Gayle stared at him. 'You think she was murdered, don't you?'

'I do, but,' he said, looking directly at Lady Gayle, 'I rather wonder if she was the intended target.'

CHAPTER TEN

'What can you mean, doctor?' Lady Gayle returned to her armchair by the fire. She slumped in the chair, giving Alice a quick glance. Shivering, she rubbed her arms, where the skin was cold and clammy.

'Lady Sylvia was wearing one of your riding habits, wasn't she?'

'Yes, but I don't see how that is of any significance. They all look pretty much the same in any case.'

'Do you not?' Dr Sloane perched himself on the edge of the armchair opposite her ladyship. 'Consider this. She was on your horse, wearing your clothes when she was shot.'

Lady Gayle swallowed, although her mouth was dry. She sipped a little brandy, ignoring the doctor's frown. 'She was, but I'm not convinced that means the bullet was meant for me.' She pulled a shawl around her shoulders. 'I think I'd like to be alone now, doctor,' she said. Her thoughts were racing, and she needed a moment alone to think about who would want to kill Lady Sylvia.

Dr Sloane rose. 'Very well. I will leave these powders for you. Take them only if you have difficulty sleeping.' He gathered his medical bag and gave a curt nod before leaving.

Lady Gayle sipped more of the brandy. Then, hanging her head, she turned to Alice. 'I'm exhausted. I think I'd like some coffee,' she said. 'And maybe some toast.'

'Cook is preparing an early breakfast,' Alice replied. 'Would you care for a tray, or would you prefer to go down to the dining room?'

'A tray,' she murmured, wandering to the window, and staring outside. Dawn was breaking on the horizon, shafts of sunlight beginning to creep over the hedges and lawns of the formal garden. As she watched, the pale gold glimmer turned orange. She twisted around at a cough behind her.

Alice had placed a tray on the low table near the fire. Delicious smells wafted in her direction, and she salivated.

'Thank you, Alice.'

Alice poured coffee, and her ladyship sipped at it, noticing the warmth ease through her body. Will I ever be warm again? she wondered. But she cast her mind back to other cold days, to the time when her ambulance broke down near the Western Front. Unable to move, her patient had died from cold, and she and her co-driver had nearly joined him. If it had not been for meeting Corporal Chadwick and his small patrol of men, there was no telling what may have happened. Afterwards, Lady Gayle was determined to learn more about engines and how to fix them, so she'd never be caught out like that again.

She turned her attention to the silver dome covering a plate. Underneath were sausages, eggs, and bacon. And a tomato. Where Cook had found a tomato at this time of year was beyond her understanding. Lady Gayle carried the tray to her dressing table, sat down and ate her fill. Later, despite the coffee, she gave into her exhausted state and retired to her bed for a lie down. Alice drew the heavy curtains, and Lady Gayle lay in the dark, her mind racing. She knew she would not sleep again until she had discovered what had happened to poor Lady Sylvia.

She was wrong.

It was early afternoon when she woke. Alice was drawing back the thick brocade curtains, and light flooded into the room. Lady Gayle sat up, blinking back guilty tears. *How can I have slept while Lady Sylvia lies dead below stairs?*

'A detective inspector from Scotland Yard has arrived, milady. He's called Aubrey Coward.' Alice bobbed and lay fresh clothes over a stand near the fire. 'I have brought hot water for you. Will you see him this afternoon?'

'Tell him I'll be down directly, Alice.' Lady Gayle swung her legs to the floor and found that she was able to stand easily. She completed her toilette and dressed herself, delighted to find that Alice had also organised a tray of sandwiches for her. 'How can I be so hungry?' she murmured.

She found Inspector Aubrey Coward in the library.

He was pacing in front of the fire, a tall, slender man who twisted his hat in his hands. 'Your ladyship,' was all he said when he saw her.

She glanced at the tortured hat, wondering why he'd not given it to Fredericks, who stood poised to rescue the item. 'Good afternoon. Mr Coward, is it? I trust you had a good journey?'

'My name is *Inspector* Coward, your ladyship. I took the express and arrived a while ago. I was told you were sleeping. I trust you are now well rested?' He dropped his hat onto the sofa.

Lady Gayle dipped her head briefly whilst trying to ignore the agonised expression on her butler's face. When she raised her head, the inspector's light grey eyes bored into her soul.

'I've been to see where the accident took place,' he said, continuing to pace back and forth. 'I would like you to tell me what happened when you discovered the body. Is now convenient?'

Lady Gayle sat on the sofa. 'Tea, Inspector?' she said, determined not to be irritated or alarmed by the pacing man. She bit back a smile when she saw Fredericks retrieve the trilby hat and pat it into shape as he left the room. *Why is the inspector so anxious?* Perhaps it's his first murder case, she decided, shaking her head as she poured tea from the exquisitely decorated pot.

The inspector did not miss the action. 'I really don't have time for tea,' he said, but all the same, he took a cup from her hand and dropped onto the sofa facing her. 'What can you tell me?'

Lady Gayle reported the events of the day before. She regarded the inspector as he placed the cup down and made notes in a small black book. She noted how fast he wrote and wondered if he'd be able to read his notes later.

'Lady Sylvia was wearing one of your riding habits. Was that normal?'

'She had not brought one of her own with her. We have several here. My maid found where they had been stored in the attics. She retrieved one for me and then discovered another one for Lady Sylvia when I asked her to look for one.'

'Why was Lady Sylvia riding alone? Surely, if she was your guest, you would show her around the estate?'

'I was called back to the house by my mother. She wanted to speak to me about something.'

'Which was?'

Lady Gayle took a deep breath. She was unused to being questioned in this manner. 'I don't know, Inspector. When I returned, mama said she'd not asked me to come back at all. I meant to find out more about it, but I forgot.'

'It could have been a ploy to get you out of the way and leave Lady Sylvia alone,'' the inspector said, scribbling more notes. 'Was Lady Sylvia a competent rider?'

Lady Gayle nodded. 'I would not have left her to ride alone if I thought there was any risk to her safety.'

'And there have been no other unusual occurrences recently?'

Lady Gayle hesitated, and the inspector looked up from his notebook. He tapped his pencil on the open page.

'There have been some odd noises at night, mostly from the attics, but Bethencourt Castle is an ancient house. There are often strange noises.'

'I'd like to see these attics,' said the inspector. He picked up his cup and drank some tea. A flicker of annoyance passed over his face.

'Is that necessary, Inspector?' said Lady Gayle. 'They have no bearing on Lady Sylvia's death.'

'It's a murder, your ladyship, and I like to be thorough,' he replied, looking around for his hat.

'Very well.' Lady Gayle approached the tea tray. 'Would you like a fresh cup, Inspector?'

He rose and shook his head. 'Attics,' he replied. 'If you would be so good, your ladyship.'

Lady Gayle stood. 'Mr Fredericks, the butler can show

you.' She pulled the bell rope, and Fredericks immediately strode into the room. 'Fredericks, the inspector would like to see the attics. Could someone escort him?'

Fredericks bowed. 'At once, my lady.'

'That won't be necessary,' the inspector announced. 'I still have questions. We can continue with my questions as we walk, your ladyship.'

Lady Gayle glanced at Fredericks, her eyes widening. The butler's face was impassive, although his eyes narrowed at the inspector. He glided to the door and held it open, bowing slightly as her ladyship strolled past, determined not to be rushed by the police.

CHAPTER ELEVEN

With Inspector Coward hot on her heels, Lady Gayle swept up the grand staircase at the centre of the hall. At the top, she headed down a corridor and through a small door. These were the back stairs used by the domestic staff and were rarely frequented by any of the family. Even so, they were swept clean but were narrower than the public stairs. Lady Gayle was well aware of the inspector's proximity as they climbed three flights before they arrived in the corridor leading to the attics.

The dusting was less apparent here, and there were scuff marks where surely Alice had walked to collect the riding habits.

'Who has been up here recently?' said the inspector.

'Just my maid.'

'Are you sure? There are two sets of footprints,' replied Inspector Coward.

'Perhaps that's the ghost.'

Inspector Coward peered at her in the low light. 'Ghost?'

'Yes, the first Earl Bethencourt is said to haunt the castle.'

'I see,' replied the inspector. 'These are both women's footprints. See the small size of the marks made? Unlikely to be your ghost unless he had very small feet.'

'Perhaps my maid asked one of the other maids to accompany her to show her which trunk to find the riding habits in. She's not used to the countryside either and finds the house rather trying,' said Lady Gayle. 'I, of course, used to play up here a great deal when I was a child, and we were invited to stay by Uncle Percival.'

'We?'

'Yes, my parents, my brother, and I. We were often invited to spend time here during the summer months.' A smile ghosted across her face at the childhood memories.

'Why hasn't your brother inherited the estate?'

Lady Gayle whirled around and glared at him. 'Why on earth do you think, Inspector?'

'I'm sorry.' He dipped his head, and his ears reddened.

Many young men had not returned from the conflict, and Alfred, her beloved brother, had been amongst them. Lady Gayle strode to the door ahead and wrenched it open. Several trunks lay on the floor, and Lady Gayle marched to the one that appeared to be the most recently disturbed. She jerked the lid open, but it was empty.

'This must have held the riding habits that Alice fetched for me.' Lady Gayle wrinkled her nose at the stench of mothballs and dropped the lid. The clatter resounded loudly throughout the attic room.

Inspector Coward jumped and knocked into another trunk. He bit back a yelp, glaring at the source of the noise with clenched fists.

Lady Gayle began to laugh, thinking he deserved the fright after his thoughtless remark about her brother, but one look at his pale face made her bite back her mirth. She'd seen shellshock before, and it was no laughing matter. 'I'm sorry,' she said. 'I didn't realise. My cousins were always playing pranks up here. It reminded me of happier times.'

'I don't wear a badge advertising my condition,' he snapped as he rose and brushed dust and cobwebs from his suit. 'I was discharged in 1917.'

'I'm sorry,' she repeated.

'You said.' He tugged at the lapels of his suit jacket and brushed himself down. 'Was there anything in that trunk?'

'No, only mothballs. The other trunks look untouched. I should have asked Alice to bring you up here. She would know more. I've not been in the attics since I was a child.'

Inspector Coward took his notebook from his pocket and began scribbling again. His pencil flew over the page, and Lady Gayle edged closer. The notebook was covered in illegible squiggles.

'How on earth can you read that?' she said.

'Shorthand,' he replied. 'I decided to learn it after the war. It's a very useful skill.'

'I can imagine,' she said. 'Was there anything else you wanted to see here? Perhaps the ghost?'

'There is no ghost,' he said. 'How many ghosts need bread and cheese to survive?' He pointed to the other side of the trunk he'd slammed into. On the floor, there was a metal plate and an enamel mug. Water from the mug he had knocked over had trickled onto the floor.

Lady Gayle placed her hands on her hips and frowned. 'I see what you mean. Someone must be hiding up here.

And someone else is keeping it a secret. I will discuss it with Mr Fredericks.'

Inspector Coward again followed her ladyship on the return journey to the library.

She was deep in thought about discovering his shell-shock, and she jumped when he spoke.

'Are you up to seeing the body?' he said. 'I would not normally ask a lady to view something so distressing, but I understand you were a nurse during the war?'

'I was an ambulance driver, then I learned about engines, but yes, Inspector, I have seen my fair share of trauma. Lady Sylvia, however... she was a friend and...'

'I do understand. As I said, I would not normally ask—'

'What do you need me to do, Inspector?'

'I would like you to tell me how she was lying when you found her. I normally like to see the body in situ, but that wasn't possible in this case.'

'It was not, but you said that you visited the site, did you not? I can, however, give you a full explanation without needing to see the body.' Lady Gayle drew her shoulders back and clenched her jaw.

'Sometimes it helps to jog the memory.'

'I am hardly likely to forget the events of yesterday evening, Inspector, but if you insist.'

Inspector Coward strolled to the door and held it open for her. 'I am most grateful, your ladyship,' he said.

Lady Gayle found herself following him to the cold room near the kitchen. It was a windowless room built with thick walls of Yorkshire stone. A sheet-covered bench stood in the centre of the room. Lady Gayle hovered in the doorway. The bedsheet silhouetted the outline of her friend.

Inspector Coward carefully rolled back the sheet, revealing Sylvia's ashen face. Under the light from the torches held in wall sconces, Sylvia's face seemed almost blue. Her lips were purple, and the gash on her head, although cleaned by a careful hand, was deep and wide. A bruise had formed on Sylvia's otherwise perfect cheek.

Tears pricked Lady Gayle's eyes, and she blinked them away before facing the inspector. 'What do you want to know,' she growled.

'I appreciate that it was dark when you found Lady Sylvia, but how was she lying?'

'On her back, her head was twisted to the left. I presume the rock she hit her head on caused that.' Lady Gayle indicated the gash on her friend's head.

The inspector peered at the gash. 'It seems likely,' he said. 'What else did you notice?'

'She was cold, but I ran my hands over her to try and find the injury. I reached underneath her, and then I felt the blood on my fingertips.' Lady Gayle stepped closer to the bench. The hole in the riding habit was clearer now, even though the light was not much better here than it had been by the brook. Fascinated, Lady Gayle gazed at the wound. So small and insignificant, she thought.

'Did you turn her body over?'

'No, Inspector, there wasn't enough space beside the brook. I tried to find a pulse but was unable to. I could feel all the blood, and I know a thing or two about gunshot wounds from my time in the war. I thought the best action was to fetch help.'

Lady Gayle turned to walk from the cold room. At the door, she hesitated and turned around. 'What happened to the rose?'

'Rose?' repeated Inspector Coward.

'Yes, a bouquet of late roses was sent yesterday morning. I pinned a rose on each of us. Just here.' Lady Gayle's hand shook as she touched the lapel of her blouse. She had pinned the pale pink rose on exactly the same spot where the rifle bullet had pierced her friend's chest.

CHAPTER TWELVE

'Who sent the flowers?' Again, the inspector whipped out his notebook and pencil.

'I have no idea. I don't believe that there was a note, but one of the servants may know.' Lady Gayle shivered and rubbed her arms. 'If you have finished here, Inspector, might we return to the warm?' She glanced at the bench one last time, wanting to be as far from Lady Sylvia's body as she could get.

'Naturally, your ladyship.' Inspector Coward whisked back the curtain which covered the exit. Even as she stepped into the warmth of the kitchen, she felt relieved.

'May I get you a cup of tea, your ladyship?' Mrs Wood rushed over; concern etched across her ruddy face.

The inspector nodded. Cook turned around and signalled to the kitchen maid. Tea was soon brought over with freshly baked biscuits. Despite knowing she was encroaching on the downstairs domain, Lady Gayle sat at the scrubbed table and ate ravenously.

What is wrong with me, she wondered. *Why am I so*

hungry? She choked on a biscuit, worried about her sudden gluttony. *This isn't normal behaviour, is it?*

'The roses?' Inspector Coward took a place on the bench next to her. He seemed oblivious to the glares of the kitchen staff who would never have sat beside her ladyship, let alone sit in her company, without express permission.

Lady Gayle closed her eyes. When she and Lady Sylvia had descended to the hall, the flowers were resting on the table. There was no card as far as she could recall, which was why she had assumed that the flowers were intended for her. She'd asked Fredericks for scissors and snipped a rose for herself and one for Lady Sylvia. *Had one of them made a joke about them looking like twins?* She couldn't remember. They had bustled happily to the stables and the awaiting horses. Then, there was the demand from her mother that she should return to the castle for some errand or another. The rest of the morning was spent attending to paperwork sent by Mr Southall. Lunch and then the news that Plantagenet had returned without Lady Sylvia.

'Did you quarrel?' The inspector's voice cut across her reverie.

'I beg your pardon?' Lady Gayle gazed at him as if trying to recall quite who he was.

'You and Lady Sylvia, did you quarrel about anything? The attentions of a young man, perhaps? Who the intended recipient of the roses was?'

'No, nothing like that. I was happy to see her, and she was happy to be here, away from London and her life there. She sent me a telegram. In it, she said it was all too much and that she needed a break.'

'Were you aware that she was due to marry Viscount Charles Vickery?'

'Yes, I was. She told me the night she arrived. I don't see

what that has to do with anything. I was very happy for her.'

'Wasn't Viscount Vickery one of your beaus before the war?' Inspector Coward tilted his head with a quizzical expression.

'How on earth do you know that? Viscount Vickery and I were good friends once, but he didn't make me an offer of marriage. Then, I met Viscount Sexton during the war, and I married him. Lady Sylvia and I had no quarrels over men.'

'That's not what I've heard,' said the inspector.

'I'd like to know who you have been speaking to.' Lady Gayle folded her arms.

Inspector Coward made several squiggles in his notebook. 'Do you have any enemies, Lady Gayle?'

'No, of course not. Well, none that I can think of.'

'Did you not have a disagreement with one of your neighbours recently?'

'Oh, that.' Lady Gayle gave an unladylike snort. 'Yes, I did disagree with Colonel Gosforth over some land. It's a good fishing spot, and he insists that he should have it back. It was lost in a game of cards, you see.'

'I take a dim view of gambling, Lady Gayle,' sniffed the inspector.

'It took place long before I was born,' snapped Lady Gayle, more than a little exasperated. 'I really don't think that I can be held responsible for events which took place last century.'

'All the same, I think I will depart now and speak with your neighbour, Colonel Gosforth.'

Lady Gayle rose from the kitchen bench.

'Alone, your ladyship. I will speak with the colonel alone.'

'Very well. Fredericks, could you ask Chadwick to bring the car around?'

Inspector Coward left the comfort of the kitchen and sat on a hard chair in the hall until the car arrived. When Fredericks opened the door, the inspector walked outside to stand on the portico. He whistled when he saw that the car was a Bentley. The chauffeur leapt out and opened the rear door; it was only as he bent down to step inside the vehicle that he realised Lady Gayle Summer was already ensconced on the back seat.

'I had planned to see Colonel Gosforth on my own,' muttered Inspector Coward.

'It would be very remiss of me to send you over there without an introduction. It is, after all, the neighbourly thing to do.'

'What makes you think that I would need an introduction?'

Lady Gayle glanced at him. She didn't like the smug expression on his face. *No, I don't like that at all. What is he playing at?* She pulled the car rug tightly around her knees, leaving the inspector, his legs covered only in his city trousers, to freeze.

As the Bentley wound down the driveway to the park gates, Lady Gayle allowed her mind to drift. It was only a few days ago that she had buried her father, and now, here she was, on the verge of burying her friend. She sniffed and was surprised when the inspector offered her a clean handkerchief. She waved it away and opened her small bag to retrieve the lacy square that Alice had placed in there.

She thought long and hard about the bouquet of roses as they lay on the table in the hall. Such a glorious shade of pink to be found in the middle of winter.

Closing her eyes, she racked her brain. *No, I'm sure there wasn't a card. I was sure they were for me, but perhaps they were for Sylvia after all.*

Did anyone know that Sylvia was staying with her at Bethencourt? Charles, of course, it made sense that Charles would know. But wouldn't he also know that Sylvia favoured white roses? It was she who loved the pink blooms, and naturally, Charles knew that they were her favourites.

Blast, she thought. The roses are important. I'm not sure how, but I am convinced that they are.

CHAPTER
THIRTEEN

It was a few miles by road to the entrance of Lockington Court. The small manor house stood in several acres of parkland. Although not as grand as Bethencourt Castle, it was a pleasant house with tall, mullioned windows and smaller attic windows glinting from above the roof line. The gravel crunched under the car wheels as Chadwick drew the vehicle to a halt. He opened the door for her ladyship and her guest. As they approached the front door, it was opened by the colonel himself. Lady Gayle remembered that they were now keeping a very small staff since the war. Despite what the colonel thought, Lady Gayle was well versed with the reasons for the increased cost of living and the new impoverishment of her own class.

Colonel Gosforth was beaming and held out his hands towards the inspector. 'My dear chap,' he exclaimed. 'How good it is to see you again. Are you fully recovered?'

Lady Gayle snapped her jaw shut as it was in danger of becoming slack with surprise. The colonel gave her a brief nod as he shook hands with the inspector and clapped him on the shoulder.

Mrs Gosforth, however, had the good manners to welcome Lady Gayle to their home. 'Shall we leave the gentlemen to talk alone?' she said.

'I would prefer to be present,' said Lady Gayle. 'Since they will be talking about my dear friend. Especially after you made me see her body.'

Mrs Gosforth gasped audibly. 'What an awful thing for you to see, my dear.'

'That isn't quite how we conduct ourselves at Scotland Yard, your ladyship,' replied Inspector Coward. 'I must speak to the colonel in private.'

'Oh, no matter, my dear chap,' said the colonel. 'There's nothing that I can say that her ladyship cannot hear. Let us go into the drawing room. Elizabeth, could you arrange for tea to be served? I'm sure *you* don't want to be present.'

Mrs Gosforth, flustered, did as she was bid. Tea arrived but was not accompanied by the lady of the house.

The colonel poured the tea, thrusting a cup in the direction of Lady Gayle with bad grace. 'This is a very brave young man,' he said to her. 'First over the top, followed by all his men.'

Inspector Coward had the goodness to blush. 'I nearly got us all killed,' he said blandly.

'Yes, well, it was a bad business that.' The colonel dipped his head but then looked Inspector Coward in the eye. 'Now, what can I do for you, Captain Coward? I don't have a lot of time.'

'It's Inspector Coward these days, sir,' said the inspector. He glanced in Lady Gayle's direction. 'I'm sure you heard that a guest of Lady Gayle's was shot yesterday. She fell from her horse and died.'

'Yes, I know all about that,' blustered the colonel. 'Can't

keep anything quite in the country. Bunch of old windbags, the lot of them.'

'Indeed, sir. Now, could you tell me what you were doing on Tuesday?' The notebook made another appearance.

Lady Gayle noticed the colonel looking askance at it.

'Me?' he said. 'Dash it all, man, what on earth has this unfortunate incident got to do with me?'

'Were you, perhaps, inspecting your grounds, sir? Did you take a gun out? I saw a particularly fine cock pheasant burst from the hedgerow as we drove past.' The inspector said.

'Yes, I think perhaps I did. After lunch, just for a stroll. Took the twelve bore with me. Just in case, you know.'

'I don't, sir. I've always been a town man myself. Just in case of what?'

'Well, you must come and stay after this nonsense is over. I have a spare gun I can loan you. If you can cope, that is?' The colonel suddenly looked worried. 'I'm sorry, old chap. I haven't overstepped the mark, have I?'

'No, of course not, but I do prefer to stay away from sudden noises if I can.'

'Yes, yes, of course,' replied the colonel. He shifted in his chair, his face growing pink.

Heat flooded Lady Gayle's cheeks, and she avoided Inspector Coward's grim countenance as he glanced in her direction.

'Returning to the events of the day before yesterday,' he said to the colonel. 'You took a stroll in your grounds with a shotgun. Did anyone see you? Did you see anyone?'

The colonel shook his head. 'I didn't trespass on Bethencourt Castle land if that's what you're asking. Really,

Coward, I would have expected better of you. Can't you take the word of a gentleman?'

Lady Gayle glanced at the inspector. No, she thought, he's not going to take anyone's word, is he? He wants evidence. Despite herself, she admired his fortitude.

'If you should be questioning anyone, it should be this young lady. Ask her how she came to inherit the castle so quickly after her great uncle's death. Ask her how her own father died. Wasn't he thrown from the same horse? Something of a coincidence, what?'

Inspector Coward snapped his head around to look at Lady Gayle. He raised his eyebrows in askance.

Looking directly at Inspector Coward, Lady Gayle said, 'My father died of a heart attack, as well Colonel Gosforth knows. He had had a weak heart for many years and was seen regularly by Dr Sloane. Yes, he fell from the horse. Initially, it was thought it was because his heart had given out, although he survived a few more days. In utter agony, I might add. His death was sudden but not a complete surprise.'

White-faced, she rose, clenching her fists and daring her knees to give way. 'I think I should leave you gentlemen to your discussion,' she said. 'Should I send the Bentley back to convey you to the village, Inspector?'

'No need,' said the colonel. 'Captain Coward will stay here with me.'

Lady Gayle swept from the room, opening both the drawing room and the front door for herself.

Once outside, Chadwick leapt from the driver's seat and handed her into the car. He didn't ask about the inspector.

'Home please, Chadwick,' was all Lady Gayle was able to say.

He touched the shiny peak of his cap and silently complied.

Once back at Bethencourt Castle, Lady Gayle rushed to her room, where she leapt onto the bed and began punching a pillow.

'Milady,' whispered Alice as she came to attend her mistress. 'Are you unwell?'

Lady Gayle pushed herself into a sitting position and hugged the pillow to her chest. 'I'm simply angry,' she said. 'Inspector Coward and Colonel Gosforth served together in the Great War, and the colonel has as good as accused me of killing my father for the title and the castle.'

'I see,' said Alice. She removed her ladyship's shoes and rubbed her feet. 'Were you suspicious at all at how soon Lord Cedric died?'

'Not at the time, but I am now,' said her ladyship. 'What on earth can I do though? If Colonel Gosforth has his way, he'll see me hanged for Lady Sylvia's death and possibly for my father's too. What an odious man he is.'

Alice laughed. 'Which man do you mean, milady?'

Lady Gayle sniffed. 'Probably both of them,' she replied.

'Then, milady,' replied Alice. 'We will have to find out who the real killer is for ourselves, won't we?'

CHAPTER
FOURTEEN

'THAT'S AN ABSOLUTELY SPLENDID IDEA,' SAID LADY GAYLE. SHE jumped to her feet. 'I know I'll not leap to conclusions about any evidence.' It would be just like working out what was wrong with an engine. Listen to it running; ears pricked for the scratch, squeak, or rumble of the sick machine. It was all she could do not to leap up and dance with glee.

'It will be such fun,' she said, pacing at the foot of her bed. 'The first thing we need to do is find out who sent those flowers. Were they meant for me, or did I make a mistake and they were meant for Lady Sylvia?'

'Very good, milady. But who would know she'd be riding Plantagenet?'

'No one. That's a very good point, Alice.' Lady Gayle halted, folding her arms.

'And who would want Lady Sylvia dead? There must be a motive.'

Lady Gayle squinted at her maid. 'Alice, have you been reading Mrs Christie's book again? I told you it would give you nightmares.'

All the same, Alice was right. *People don't kill without a reason, do they?* 'Felicity Makepeace,' she said at last. 'Lady Sylvia said she wasn't happy about the engagement with Viscount Vickery.'

'Could it have been Miss Makepeace who shot her ladyship?' Alice was wide-eyed, her face red with excitement.

Lady Gayle was caught up in the moment, and then she sat down. Her good friend Lady Sylvia was dead, and here she was behaving as if it were something to be excited about. She sat at her dressing table and began to brush her hair, gazing at herself in the mirror, when Fredericks announced that Inspector Coward had returned. She relinquished the brush to Alice with a sigh. She was still becoming used to having a full-time maid, and Alice was so much more efficient with her hair than she was.

'No, Alice, I don't think it was Miss Makepeace. Anyway, I'd better see what the inspector wants now.'

'I have put him in the library, my lady,' said Fredericks. 'The Dowager Countess is in the drawing room. Shall I bring tea?'

Lady Gayle rose and slipped her shoes on before checking her hair in the mirror. She nodded her thanks to Alice. 'No, no tea, thank you, Fredericks. I thought he was staying with the colonel. I can't imagine what he wants now. Did he say?'

'Not to me, my lady.' Fredericks gave his usual half-bow before opening the bedroom door for her.

She strode along the hallway and down the stairs, heading towards the library. Movement in the gallery caught her eye, and she turned in time to see a black-clad maid dart away. *What on earth is she doing?* Lady Gayle stopped for a moment. There were only family portraits hung there. Lord Percival's sons both painted at age sixteen.

She gave a wistful smile, remembering the boys they had been. How she and her brother Alfred had loved their summers here at the castle.

When she reached the library, Inspector Coward was nowhere to be seen. *Dash it all, man. Haven't I got enough to do without chasing you around?* She went back to the door, but Fredericks was already opening it.

'The inspector is outside on the portico, my lady.'

'What on earth is he doing there?'

Fredericks never allowed anything to disconcert him, and today was no different. 'I really couldn't say, my lady, but he did ask me to fetch you.'

'Am I some lap dog to be collected at his whim? No, don't answer that, Fredericks.' She marched to the door, grabbing the coat offered by the butler, wrapping it around herself as she stepped outside. 'Back so soon, Inspector?' she said. 'I thought you were staying with Colonel Gosforth?'

Inspector Coward was peering at one of the ochre pillars with a magnifying glass in his hand. If he heard her question, he ignored it.

Lady Gayle watched him whilst wondering if looking like the fictional detective, Sherlock Holmes, was merely for effect. 'Inspector?' she repeated, placing her hands on her hips.

He said nothing but handed her the magnifying glass and pointed at a spot on the pillar.

She raised the glass to her eye and peered through it. She straightened and passed the glass back. 'Enlighten me,' she said.

'It looks like a bullet hole to me,' he replied. 'However, that's not the reason for my visit. I would like to take some of your father's heart powders for testing.'

Lady Gayle shook her head and touched the ochre pillar. Something niggled at the back of her mind, but feeling the biting chill of the day, she stepped back into the hall and headed towards the library. Once she had composed herself and was warming her hands by the fire, she asked, 'Why do you need to test my father's medicine?'

'I have some unanswered questions,' he said. 'Nothing more.'

Lady Gayle gave the merest of shrugs. She rang the bell. 'Fredericks, the inspector wants Lord Cedric's heart powders. Do we have any left?'

She noticed a hint of movement around the butler's eyebrows before he replied in the affirmative.

'I will send someone to fetch them immediately,' he said.

CHAPTER FIFTEEN

A week after Lady Sylvia's death, the inquest was held in Malton, a town a few miles from Bethencourt Castle. Lady Ethel, the Dowager Countess, was incensed when she discovered she, too, had been called as a witness.

'I have never heard such nonsense,' she exclaimed.

Lady Gayle attempted to calm her as much as she could. It even occurred to her to give her mother a drop or two of the sedative that Dr Sloane had prescribed after Sylvia's death. Still, she knew from personal experience of the drug that there was a high likelihood that her mother would fall asleep and snore through the entire proceedings. Annoying as she found her mother on occasion, she felt unable to ruin Mama's reputation to that extent. She hadn't yet told her mother that the inquest would be held in the largest room of the public house, the King's Head.

Alice accompanied them, sitting on the box seat at the front of the Bentley next to the chauffeur. Although she could see them chatting away, Lady Gayle was unable to hear the conversation. She had been brought up not to eavesdrop on people's conversations, but she found herself itching to know what was being said.

Next to her, her mother grumbled about the cold, the inconvenience, and the indignity of attending a court. Lady Gayle pulled the thick black veil over her face and closed her eyes.

Chadwick stopped the Bentley outside the front of the King's Head, and Lady Ethel found herself being escorted inside by her daughter a little more rapidly than she was used to. The main parlour had been set out as much like a courtroom as possible. Lady Gayle was annoyed to see Colonel Gosforth chatting so amiably with Dr Sloane and Major Edlington, the local magistrate and coroner.

She found a seat for herself and her mother and waited for the proceedings to begin. There had been an inquest into her father's death as it had been so sudden, but he was found to have died from injuries suffered due to his fall from the eighteen-hand grey horse.

Finding herself watching the process with interest, Lady Gayle did not notice Inspector Coward stroll into the room until he raised his hat to her. She glanced at him and looked away. She had not seen him since the day when he returned from Lockington Court and demanded her father's heart medication for testing. She clenched her fists, feeling her short nails bite into the palms of her hands. It was the only way to maintain control of her fear and her temper.

One after the other, witnesses were sworn in and gave their evidence. Eventually, it was her turn, and she was glad she'd worn an old pre-war frock so that no one could see how much her knees were shaking.

Placing her hand on the bible, she promised to be truthful.

Major Edlington took her gently through the preliminary questions. Confirming her name, her title and where she resided.

'When did Lady Redmond-Smythe come to Bethencourt Castle, your ladyship?'

'I received a letter from her on Saturday the fourth of November. She said she was rather fed up with London and asked if she could come to stay. I replied, yes, of course, and she arrived a few days later.'

'That would be the week commencing the sixth of November?'

'No, Major, it was just after my father's funeral. Lady Sylvia arrived on the fifteenth.'

'What happened after then?'

'We dined together and went to bed early, having arranged to take the horses out. I left word for Mr Shepherd to have the horses ready for eleven o'clock. In the morning, we had breakfast on trays in our rooms; well, at least I did. I believe Lady Sylvia did the same. We met in the hallway a little before the appointed time.'

'What happened then?'

'We went to the stables. Oh, no. I'm forgetting. There was a delivery of roses. They arrived on the early train. We each took a rose and pinned it to our jackets.'

'Lady Sylvia pinned the rose to her own lapel?'

Lady Gayle dipped her head. 'No, that's not quite right. I pinned a rose to myself, and then a rose onto Lady Sylvia.'

'Very good,' replied the major. 'Please continue.'

'When we arrived at the stables, I had a message from the Dowager Countess that she required me back at the house. I told Lady Sylvia to take my horse, Plantagenet, and wished her a pleasant ride.'

'You and Lady Sylvia did not at that time exchange words?'

'Only the words that I have told you.'

'You did not, for example, exchange harsh words about Viscount Vickery?'

'No, Major, we did not! I have already explained this to Inspector Coward.'

'And no harsh words were exchanged the night before on the same subject?'

'No, Major. I don't know who has given you this information, but I can assure you it is a lie.'

'Thank you, your ladyship. What happened after Lady Sylvia rode off alone?'

'I returned to the house, spoke briefly to my mother, and discovered she had not asked me to return to the house. Since she did not need me, I went to my father's study. I wrote some letters and read through some paperwork that had been left for me by Mr Southall.'

'Are there any witnesses to your being in the study?'

'I couldn't say, Major. Perhaps I was brought some tea or coffee during the morning. I don't recall. Later, I joined my mother for lunch. Both Fredericks and Owens can attest to that.'

'Very good, my lady. That will be all.'

Lady Gayle returned to her seat next to her mother.

'I call Dowager Countess Bethencourt to the stand.'

With a rustle of stiffened silk, Lady Ethel rose to her feet. She glided to the table near Major Edlington like a ship in full sail. She was taken through similar questions to those asked of her daughter.

Then Major Edlington said, 'I only have one more question for you, Lady Ethel, when you called your daughter to return to the house instead of riding out with her friend, what did you want to discuss with her?'

'I do not have the slightest idea what you are talking about, my good man. I did not ask my daughter to return to the house. Not that day nor any other day.'

CHAPTER
SIXTEEN

There was a collective gasp in the courtroom as the attendees took in this information.

'If you did not ask your daughter to return to the house, my lady, do you know who may have done?'

The Dowager Countess held her pince-nez to her narrowed eyes. 'I do not,' she replied. 'I rather think that's a matter for you to uncover, don't you?'

With that, she swept from the room. Major Edlington rose to demand her return, but the clerk returned empty-handed. The major collapsed back into his chair, pinching the bridge of his nose between thumb and forefinger.

Trying to cover her ears from the buzzing of outraged bees resounding in her head, Lady Gayle rose to follow her mother. She had taken only two steps when her vision blurred. She grasped the wooden railing and held on. Despite feeling dizzy, she had two questions racing through her mind. She knew her mother hadn't called her back to the house and remembered discussing it with her on the day. Which meant someone else needed Lady Sylvia to be alone. Who would want that, and why? She recollected Dr

Sloane's suggestion that Lady Sylvia may not have been the intended victim. *But if that's the case, why not let us ride out together and shoot me?* No, she decided, poor Sylvia's death must have been the plan. There is no other explanation. A random thought about Felicity Makepeace sprinted through her mind, and her blood froze.

She pushed her way out of the makeshift courtroom into the main bar. 'Where is the Dowager Countess?' she asked.

'Outside in the car, milady,' said Alice.

Lady Gayle glanced around at the faces. She felt cornered and wanted to rush out.

Dr Sloane observed her behaviour and was the most reassuring. 'We need to get you away from here,' he said. 'Back to the castle. No prying eyes there.'

Lady Gayle nodded. 'Very well,' she said. As she walked from the public house, the bulb of a camera flash exploded in her face, blinding her. She took a step backwards and almost fell. She would not have made it to the car without Alice and the doctor. As soon as the door closed, Alice jumped in the front next to Chadwick, who already had the engine running. The wheels of the Bentley squealed as they pulled away.

Lady Gayle accepted the silver flask that Alice passed to her through the glass partition. Removing the cap, she drank some of the brandy, then glanced at her mother, who was staring out the car windows at the passing countryside.

'I need to find out who called for me, Mama. I think it may be important. Are you sure you can't think of anyone?'

'I do not know, and I think I've already made that quite clear, have I not?' Her mother wafted a fan in front of her face. The usual sign that she did not want to discuss a matter further.

'We have to talk about this, Mama,' replied Lady Gayle. 'If you didn't call me back from the stables, then who did? Someone wanted Lady Sylvia all on her own. Why?'

The fan snapped shut, and Lady Gayle felt it rap her forearm. Brandy gushed from the flask onto her dress. She tried to brush the brandy away whilst biting back the pain from her arm.

'I had hoped that we could leave all this to the police,' Lady Ethel said. Unusually, she spoke slowly as if choosing her words carefully. 'There is something amiss here. It is not at all ladylike to involve oneself in such tawdry matters, Gayle, but you have my full permission to undertake any investigations you need to. After all, hanging is dreadfully unladylike, isn't it?'

Lady Gayle dipped her head. 'Yes, Mama,' she said. A smile ghosted across her face. It was nice to have permission from the Mater, but since her neck was at risk, nothing was going to stop her from investigating what had happened to Lady Sylvia.

The rest of the journey continued in silence, but Lady Gayle's mind was racing.

Roses, riding habits, false messages. Somehow, they were all connected. But how?

When the party returned to Bethencourt Castle, Alice and Fredericks helped mother and daughter into the house. The Dowager Countess took to her room. Shuffling along behind her was Lady Sylvia's maid. After the death of her mistress, the maid hadn't known what to do with herself, and since Lady Ethel had dismissed yet another lady's maid, it made sense to keep the woman at Bethencourt Castle for the time being.

Lady Gayle strode to the library, where she knew a fire would be blazing. She dropped onto the sofa and fondled the soft ears of her late uncle's spaniel.

'Oh, what are we going to do, Molly?' she said.

Molly sat next to her on the sofa, her tail thumping rapidly. Gaspod, now allowed back into the house, rolled onto his back on the rug. Lady Gayle reached down to scratch the exposed chest and tummy.

'Come in, Alice,' said Lady Gayle, recognising the tone of the soft knock on the door. 'I suppose you want me to change so you can sponge this brandy out of my dress?'

'I do, milady, but was there anything else that you wanted to discuss?'

'Lots of things. Who sent the roses? Who called me back from the stables? Dr Sloane doesn't think Lady Sylvia was the intended victim, don't you know? He thinks because of the riding habits, we looked the same.'

'There's also your hair, milady. You are both blonde. At a distance, you both look alike.'

'Lady Sylvia was shot with a high-powered rifle,' said Lady Gayle glumly. 'I think it's unlikely the gunman would be using their naked eye—'

'So, they would have been able to see the difference? *If* you had been there too?'

'I suppose so. If they knew us both well enough.' Lady Gayle flopped back against the cushions, rubbing her eyes. 'I don't understand it. If I'm the target, that means they'll try again, and if Lady Sylvia was the target, why wait until she came here to kill her? Surely it would have been easier to do in London?'

'I really couldn't say, milady. I have asked below stairs, and no one has any idea who sent for you. Mr Owens thought the message came from Mr Fredericks. But Mr Fredericks knows nothing about it.'

Lady Gayle hung her head. 'Thank you for asking for me,' she said.

'It was my pleasure, milady. Now, shall we get you into some clean clothes?'

Lady Gayle didn't reply, but she followed her maid to her bedroom for something that smelt less like a distillery.

Sitting in front of her looking glass, she began to draft some notes of what she knew so far. There was no one who would want to see Lady Sylvia dead, as far as she knew. Unless she counted Felicity Makepeace, who she knew was a crack shot. She regarded herself in the mirror, wondering about Dr Sloane's remarks.

'Who wants *you* dead?' she muttered.

On the paper, she wrote *Next to Inherit* and underlined the words three times. Mr Southall had said that there was someone, a boy. How old was the child, and where did he come from? Was he born on the wrong side of the blanket? Lady Gayle gave herself a wry smile in the mirror. Mama would be so proud that she'd used such an old-fashioned phrase. Then she shook her head. Perhaps not. Considering what the phrase meant. If the boy were illegitimate, could he still inherit if anything happened to her? Perhaps she should make a will, as her father had done, but she wondered, who could she leave the castle and all its problems to.

Closing her eyes, she drifted to a moment in time when her father had encountered the same problem.

'Hello, Papa. Mama asked me to remind you that it's getting late. Will you be much longer?'

'I'm going over the accounts for the estate, my dear,' her father replied. He removed the wire-rimmed spectacles that made his grey eyes seem so large and rubbed his hands over his face. 'These new taxes are going to cripple us. Income tax has more than tripled to pay for the war debt.'

'Are we going to be poor, Papa?'

'Not compared to some poor souls,' he said. 'But, yes, the estate my cousin left me is not worth as much as it was twenty years ago.'

'Perhaps it will look better in the morning, Papa? I have some money of my own from Sexton,' she said.

'That's your money,' replied her father. 'Keep hold of it and be careful how you invest it. Government bonds have always been safe, but they pay so little now.'

'I understand, Papa,' she replied.

Her father replaced his spectacles. 'Do you, my dear? I do hope so. All this,' he waved his arms expansively to include the library and beyond, 'will be yours someday, and I need to teach you how to manage it.'

'Don't worry, Papa. We have plenty of time,' she said. 'Shall I tell Mama that you will join us directly?'

Papa nodded, but all the same, he turned his gaze back to the ledgers, scratching his head.

However, time was one of the things that they had not had. The following day, her father was thrown from Plantagenet and died a week later from heart failure brought about by his injuries.

Now Plantagenet had lost another rider.

Who on earth is going to be next? She picked up the chunk of plaster that had fallen from the portico pillars on the day of her father's funeral and rolled it back and forth in her hand, wondering if the inspector had been right about the bullet hole or not. Oh well, she thought, placing the plaster away in a drawer, the entire castle may yet fall around our ears, and that will put paid to all the tax and repair bills.

With that cheery idea, Lady Gayle pushed herself away from the dressing table and returned to the library and the concerns of running a large estate.

CHAPTER SEVENTEEN

ALICE'S CONSTANT YAWNING DID NOT GO UNNOTICED AS HER MAID prepared Lady Gayle's luggage for their London journey and Lady Sylvia's funeral.

'Are you not sleeping, Alice?' asked Lady Gayle.

'No, not last night, milady,' replied Alice. 'The ghost was walking. Or more like tap dancing in the attic.'

'Don't tell me you believe in the ghost now?' laughed Lady Gayle, but she thought back to her own night-time encounter with a shadowy figure and shivered. 'Did you go up and take a look?'

'I did not, milady. The very idea. I put my head under the covers and tried to ignore it. That Sarah Snodgrass, well, she slept through the whole thing. I felt like getting up and shaking her so she could be disturbed too.'

Lady Gayle smiled to herself. She was well aware that Alice had not wanted to share her room with Lady Sylvia's maid on the grounds that she suspected the other maid would snore. Sarah should have accompanied them today to return to her post in London, but somehow, the girl had ingratiated herself with the Dowager Countess and would be staying at Bethencourt Castle. For how long, though, was anybody's guess. Maids frequently failed to come up to Lady Ethel's exacting standards and did not last long.

Leaving Alice to finish the packing, Lady Gayle made her way to breakfast, but halfway down the stairs, she turned around and strode towards the back stairs and the attics.

The corridor leading to the attic rooms had been swept. The footprints which had been visible only a short time before were gone. If anyone else had walked this way, their passing had been brushed away and was no longer apparent. But why, wondered Lady Gayle.

Lady Gayle opened the door and peered around it. Oh, for goodness' sake, she told herself. *Get in there and find out what's been going on.* She had not brought a candle, but there was sufficient light during the day to see by. In the far corner, the trunks, which had been covered in dust when she showed the attic room to Inspector Coward, had been moved. Small ridges of dust rose where the trunks had been pulled forward, and there was a pool of wax grease on the floor. She opened the trunk, but there was nothing other than yellowing papers.

She pulled out a handful and sat on the floor. One by one, she ran her eyes over the leaves of paper. Letters, menus, shopping lists, a list of the game shot during a house party over fifty years ago, even a laundry list or two. She allowed the papers to fall back into the trunk. There was nothing of interest here. Why had anyone wanted to investigate in the middle of the night?

Her stomach rumbled, and she decided she had more important matters to attend to.

. . .

'Do you have everything you need, milady?' Alice cast her eye around the empty first-class train carriage.

Lady Gayle nodded. 'Thank you,' she said. 'I think I have everything I need. I'm going to try to rest. Perhaps you should do the same?'

'Very good, milady. I'll be in third class. I will see you at Kings Cross Station.'

'Thank you, Alice,' Lady Gayle replied. 'We're booked into the Astoria Hotel, and the funeral is at noon tomorrow.'

With a last check that all was in order, Alice scuttled out of the carriage. Lady Gayle hoped her maid would make it back to her seat in third class before the whistle blew. Given that it had been some time since they had been in London, Lady Gayle had given Alice the evening off.

She flicked disconsolately through the magazines which Alice had bought for her, but since she was alone in the carriage, she dug in her handbag for her little book and the notes she'd made. There'd been very little progress since last week's inquest. She brushed at the sleeve of her black dress. At least she was getting value for money out of the expenditure. Mr Howden would approve, she thought with a grimace. Every time they went through the estate accounts, he reminded her how the estate was struggling financially with increased wages and taxation.

Raising the black veil, she removed her cloche hat and smoothed her bobbed hair. She glanced at herself in the train window, patting her cheek. Was she getting thin? Although it was popular with the flappers, she wasn't sure that the skeletal look was for her.

Too cadaverous, Hugh had always said. He liked her curves, he'd said. She scanned her figure; she didn't have many curves now. After Hugh had died due to his injuries obtained in the German Spring Offensive of 1918, she'd continually lost weight. Especially after she'd lost their baby. Not that she'd really known she was pregnant, and no one apart from Alice knew the truth. Collapsing when she received the telegram, she hadn't understood what was happening to her body. It was only later that the hospital sister told her the truth. But she was told she was lucky; she would still be able to have more children. She'd wanted to shout, "Not without my husband," but of course, she kept quiet.

She stared out the window, watching the landscape change from the rugged peaks of Yorkshire through the flat lands of Lincolnshire and the fenlands. All too soon, the dark buildings of London rose high above the train, blocking out the grey day.

Once installed in the Astoria Hotel, Lady Gayle made a few phone calls to see if anyone was available to have dinner with her that evening. The majority of her calls were met with the message that her friend was away from home. *Is no one coming to the funeral tomorrow?*

Finally, as luck would have it, the only person at home that evening was Viscount Charles Vickery.

She dressed for dinner with Alice's help.

'What are your plans for this evening, Alice?' she said as her maid passed her a warm coat.

'The music hall, milady. Henry Sheridan is playing, and I've been waiting to see him.'

'I hope you have a lovely time,' replied Lady Gayle.

Alice blushed. 'I'll call a hansom cab for you, milady.' She rushed from the room.

Lady Gayle gave herself one last look in the mirror. Satisfied with how she looked, she left the house. Sitting back in the cab, she wondered how Charles would be coping with the loss of his fiancée. She had no idea if the match with Lady Sylvia was a love match or one of convenience. So many were, especially these days when choices were so sparse. She sighed. *Who would want Sylvia dead? Can I ask Charles?*

All too soon, she reached the restaurant where Charles had suggested they meet. As she handed her coat to the hat check girl, she became aware that she was the centre of attention. As she followed the maître d'hôtel into the main dining room, all chatter fell silent. People turned her way, and all eyes were upon her. Her picture had been in all the newspapers, linking her to Lady Sylvia's death. *Has she no shame,* they must be whispering. Goosebumps rose on her arms, but she refused to rub them. Refusing to allow her fellow diners the satisfaction of seeing that she was bothered by their stares.

Charles waved from across the room, a broad smile on his handsome face. All the eyes followed thus, and the low buzz of chatter resumed. Lady Gayle surmised it was all gossip about how she could be having dinner with the bereaved fiancé the night before the funeral.

Charles greeted her warmly and pulled a chair out for her, refusing to allow the waiter to do so. When he resumed his seat, he waited while the waiter poured her a glass of red wine.

Lady Gayle stared at the liquid in her glass and repressed a slight shudder.

'Are you cold, Gigi?' he said.

'No, I'm fine. It's just been a very trying time recently.' Lady Gayle picked up her glass. 'To Sylvia,' she said.

The viscount repeated the toast and sipped. The glass shook as he replaced it on the table. 'It's been a trying time here too,' he said. 'What happened, Gayle? Why was she on your horse?'

Lady Gayle shrugged. 'Nothing simpler,' she said. 'I received a message that Mama wanted me back at the house, so I gave Sylvia the better horse. You know what it's like since the war. We only have one decent horse and a couple of nags left.'

Charles nodded and drank more of his wine.

'Later, I discovered that it wasn't Mama who called me back. I still don't know who did. Dr Sloane thinks I may have been the target, but that doesn't make sense. If I were the target, why would I be asked to go back to the house?'

Charles raised his glass again and put it back on the table without drinking. 'You're suggesting someone wanted you out of the way for a clear shot at Sylvia?'

'Who would want to hurt Sylvia?' Lady Gayle nodded at the waiter who was trying to place her dinner in front of her.

Charles didn't reply until the waiter had left them. 'Felicity Makepeace,' he said eventually.

'Felicity? Sylvia told me she wasn't happy about the engagement, but is she unhappy enough to shoot Sylvia?'

'Unhappy? Is that what Sylvia told you? Felicity was furious. She bearded me in my den as soon as the announcement was printed in *The Times*. I wasn't even out of bed.' Charles drank the rest of the wine and refilled his glass before the waiter could move.

'Oh dear,' said Lady Gayle. 'Well, at least she wasn't in Yorkshire at the time of the shooting.'

'I think she may have been. She has friends in Harrogate. How far is that from your place?'

'Over thirty-five miles. She couldn't get to Bethencourt, shoot Sylvia, and get back to Harrogate in a day.'

'Couldn't she? Can you guess where she is now?' said Charles.

Lady Gayle shook her head.

'She's on her way to France to try and race that ruddy Bugatti of hers.'

CHAPTER
EIGHTEEN

Lady Gayle gasped and reached for her wine but was only successful in knocking it across the table. In amongst the furore of waiters mopping up the red liquid and changing the tablecloth, she stared at Charles in horror. If anyone could have driven that distance and returned in time for tea, it would be Felicity Makepeace, and now, she was out of reach of the police.

The following morning, Lady Gayle travelled alone in a taxi to Kensal Cemetery, where Lady Sylvia was due to be laid to rest. As she entered the small chapel, she felt a distinct chill that had nothing to do with the low temperature of a frosty day in late November.

Every person she nodded to turned their heads away. They blame me, she realised. Head held high, she took a place in a pew, trying hard not to show her dismay when no one came to sit near her. She raised her hand but changed her mind and decided to keep her black veil down, glad that it was thick enough to hide her face.

After the service, she followed the coffin to the graveside, trying hard to ignore the whispers surrounding her. Unable to maintain her bravado, she dipped her head and shuffled along to the graveside.

The mourners formed a circle around the trench in the ground, and Lady Gayle was unable to get close to the grave. Tempted to push her way into the circle, she demurred. *It is not in the least bit ladylike, and you are, after all, a lady.*

The cleric intoned the last words of the funeral rites, and Lady Gayle pulled her coat close around her body. Perhaps she should have given up on the idea of being stylish and dressed for the weather with a silk vest under her dress.

A bee whistled past her bare neck, and she brushed it away. Someone screamed, and when she looked at her glove, she realised it was covered in blood.

Then she was falling, a thump on her arm taking her off her feet. She tried to bite down the pangs of nausea as she became aware that everyone was standing around her looking down at her.

For a moment, she had the horrid feeling that she had taken Sylvia's place and that she was the corpse. Panicking, she tried to rise, but she was pushed firmly back to the ground.

'Lie still, Gigi darling,' came a voice she eventually recognised as Viscount Charles Vickery. 'You've been shot.'

The jangling of the ambulance bell edged into the periphery of her mind. Why was she lying down? Shouldn't she be at the wheel? Opening her eyes, she saw the white headdress and red cross of a nurse, concern etched across the woman's face.

'I'm glad to see you're still with us,' she said. 'Now lie still, we'll soon be at the hospital.' The nurse smoothed stands of hair away from Lady Gayle's face.

The movement reminded her of her mother doing the same to soothe her back to sleep after a nightmare. Lady Gayle closed her eyes, biting her lip every time the ambulance lurched and bounced on the cobbles. She winced as pressure was applied to her neck as she closed her eyes, recalling the funeral, the black clothes, the sombre day—the blood on her glove.

The bell ceased clanging, and the rear doors were wrenched open. Lady Gayle bit back the pain as her stretcher was dragged from the rear of the blood wagon and pulled into the hospital.

She heard voices calling from far away, fading further into the distance as she succumbed to the chloroform.

When she awoke much later, the white headdress had been replaced with a dark trilby hat. The face, albeit a different face, was etched with the same concern.

'Inspector Coward?'

'Shush,' he said. 'Don't make too much noise, or I shall be in trouble for waking you. You're supposed to be resting, but I came to make sure you were still alive.'

'I'm fine,' she said and pushed herself onto her elbows. Wincing with the pain in her left arm, she dropped back onto the bed but was unable to prevent a yelp of distress.

Rushing feet on the hard floor clattered in her direction.

'That's done it,' said the inspector. He leaned against

the wall with a stifled laugh, disappearing from her line of vision.

'Inspector, I distinctly told you not to wake my patient.'

Even without seeing the speaker, Lady Gayle recognised the voice. She groaned. It was Sister Edwards—the demon of the wards. As a young ambulance driver, she'd often found herself on the wrong side of Sister Edwards but discovered, to her surprise, that she was relieved this was the person taking care of her. Despite knowing she was in good hands, Lady Gayle bit back a shout as her uninjured arm was grabbed and her wrist held in a vicelike grip. Twisting her head to the side, she encountered the grim visage of Sister Edwards.

'It appears you will live, Miss Summer,' announced Sister Edwards. 'Although I hear I should call you Lady Gayle now. Trust you to wait for the war to be over and then get shot. At least it's only a flesh wound. You needn't make such a fuss.'

'Shot?' Lady Gayle whispered. Her voice cracked—her mouth was so dry. Sister Edwards beckoned a nurse who held a cup of water to her parched lips.

Lady Gayle drank as much as she was able, allowing the nurse to ease her head back onto the pillows.

'Five minutes,' announced Sister Edwards.

The ward echoed with the sound of her feet marching away, and then there was complete silence.

'Shot?' Lady Gayle repeated as soon as Inspector Coward's face appeared in her eyeline.

'What do you remember?' said Inspector Coward. He had removed his hat, and his grey eyes held hers.

Heat stole up her face, and she broke the gaze, closing her eyes to think or was it to gain time? *What on earth is happening to me?*

'I went to the funeral. I remember being in the chapel for the service, following the coffin outside... A bee,' she said. 'A bee flew past my ear. It must have been a large one. I felt the breeze.'

'It's November, my lady,' said Inspector Coward, with a faint smile. 'I may be a townie, but even I know that bees aren't around in November. I believe they hibernate.'

'I think you may be right, Inspector.' She opened her eyes, turning her head to stare at him. 'Who shot me?'

'I was hoping you could tell me that.' The notebook was out, the pencil poised once more. 'Who would want you dead?'

'Gosh,' she said. 'I think almost everyone at Lady Sylvia's funeral. Everyone looked daggers at me. No one spoke to me at all. It was absolutely horrid. Then we went outside, and I tried to get close to the grave, but no one would let me through.

'I say, are you absolutely sure the shot was meant for me? It could have been for one of the other mourners.'

Inspector Coward cocked his head to one side, giving her a sceptical look. 'Lady Gayle...' he began. 'You're not a fool—'

'Well thank you very much, Inspector.'

Inspector Coward flashed her a look of annoyance. 'As I was saying, you're not a fool, and I am confident you do not believe in coincidences. Are you sure there have been no other attempts on your life? What about the day Lady Sylvia was shot? Did you ever find out who sent the message asking you to come back to the house?'

'No, Inspector, I did not.'

'I don't suppose you ever will. It leaves you in a vulnerable position, doesn't it? Called away mysteriously. No independent alibi.'

'I don't think I like what you're suggesting, Inspector,' said Lady Gayle.

'Are you quite sure that Lady Sylvia was the target?'

'I honestly don't know, Inspector. I thought she was. In any case, who would want me dead?'

'What happens to the title and the estate if you should die?'

'There's a boy—if he's still alive—he's a third or maybe a fourth cousin. My solicitor mentioned him when he read my father's will. He's been trying to find out more about the child and is still trying to ascertain if the boy survived the war. He would have been old enough to serve, but he may not have lived through the war, or the Spanish flu could have killed him.'

'And after this boy?'

'The estate reverts to the crown. I can leave everything to my mother for her lifetime, but after that...' her voice trailed off. 'I'm so tired. I would prefer to discuss this later.'

'I would prefer to talk now—'

'But your five minutes are up, Inspector, and my patient needs to rest.' Sister Edwards had approached soundlessly, making them both jump.

Inspector Coward glanced at the sister. If he'd planned to say something, he rapidly changed his mind and tucked his notebook into the breast pocket of his suit jacket. Lady Gayle wanted to tell him that it spoiled the line of the material, but even as she opened her mouth to speak, she yawned, and sleep claimed her once more.

CHAPTER NINETEEN

When she woke, Lady Gayle was delighted to find her old friend Evelyn Trent seated in a chair beside her bed. She reached out her right hand to her old companion from the war years.

'How good it is to see you,' she exclaimed. 'How did you know I was here?'

'You made the newspapers. Again,' replied Evelyn, 'I had a little work to find out which hospital you were in, but I tracked you down in the end.'

'I am delighted that you did. How have you been?'

Evelyn tucked her gloves onto her lap, but not before Lady Gayle noticed how frayed they were. Even her friend's coat and hat, although clean, had seen better days.

'I am so sorry I was unable to invite you to stay at Bethencourt Castle,' she said, ashamed of her earlier decisions to refuse some house guests. 'I had received a letter from Lady Sylvia a few days beforehand, and Mama could not cope with too many visitors so soon after we lost poor Papa.'

'I quite understand. I didn't come here to talk about

that. I came to see how you are. The newspaper report suggested that someone tried to shoot you?'

'So it seems,' replied Lady Gayle. 'All stuff and nonsense naturally. Or at least I believed so, but since this,' she indicated her neck wound, 'and dear Lady Sylvia... I don't know what to think.'

Evelyn edged closer and peeked under the dressing. 'You are going to have a wonderful scar,' she said. 'If it was on your face, we could tell people it was a duelling scar. But nothing worse than that.'

Lady Gayle smiled. Evelyn's warped sense of humour had seen them through many dark days during the war. Even the constant threat of enemy fire and shell blasts did nothing to dampen Evelyn's mood as they negotiated the meat wagon, as she'd called it, past the potholes and mounds of mud.

'I would really prefer not to wear high necklines to cover it,' Lady Gayle said. 'Perhaps some extra strings of pearls.'

'I would wear it with pride if I were you. Now tell me the truth, did someone really want to kill you, and why?'

'Before I settle down and tell you everything, would you mind asking a nurse if we can have some tea from the trolley? Then you can make yourself comfortable, and I will divulge all the grisly details.' With a wince, Lady Gayle pushed herself up higher in the bed, and Evelyn plumped up her pillows before collecting a tray bearing two cups of strong-looking dark tea and a bowl of sugar.

Lady Gayle arched an eyebrow at the potent brew before spooning in extra sugar and giving the liquid a vigorous stir. She told Evelyn everything that had happened since the death of her great uncle Percival the previous Easter.

'He was an old man, and therefore, his death was not unexpected, but my father only survived him by a few months. When Lady Sylvia was killed, I think the inspector thought I'd had a hand in both deaths.'

'Does the inspector think your father was murdered?'

Lady Gayle nodded. 'I believe so. Papa had a bad heart, although he had been taking heart medication prescribed for him by Dr Sloane. When he fell from his horse and died, we all believed that it was a heart attack which caused the fall. Even Dr Sloane agreed with that conclusion. There was an autopsy, but the results were inconclusive. The examining doctor was unable to tell if a heart attack caused the fall or if injuries from the fall caused his final heart attack. The inspector has now taken father's heart preparation away for analysis.'

'The inspector believed there was foul play and suspected your involvement?' Evelyn was open-mouthed with shock.

'I believe he still suspects me.'

'Don't be silly, Gayle, now that someone has shot at you, surely you cannot still be a suspect?'

'I am sure that Inspector Coward will see this attack on me as a mere ploy, designed to remove all suspicion from me. He has a very devious mind. I honestly believe he made me look at Sylvia's body to gauge my reaction. You wait until you meet him.'

'I look forward to it,' replied Evelyn.

Lady Gayle glanced towards the glass insert in the door to her private room. 'How incredibly fortunate,' she said when she saw the inspector's face at the window. 'He's back.'

. . .

Inspector Coward glanced at Lady Gayle's visitor as he strode into her room. 'I need to speak to you in private,' he said.

'You may speak in front of my friend. Evelyn, this is Inspector Coward. Inspector, this is Evelyn Trent. We drove ambulances together during the war.'

The inspector tugged at the lapels of his heavy overcoat before removing his notebook and flicking to the correct page. 'Very well,' he began. 'I have received the analysis of your father's heart medication.' He paused. 'Would you be surprised to hear that it contained digitalis?'

'I would be more surprised if it didn't, Inspector,' replied Lady Gayle. 'Digitalis has long been used as a heart medication. In small doses, it can be very beneficial.'

Inspector Coward cocked his head. 'In small doses, yes, my lady,' he said. 'However, the strength of the digitalis in your father's medication could and, in fact, did, prove fatal.'

Lady Gayle gripped her bedding tightly, an action that did not go unnoticed by the inspector. When she saw his eyes fixed on her whitened knuckles, she tried to calm all her outward signs of panic.

'Is there anything you'd like to express about the strength of your father's heart medication, my lady? Perhaps you could tell me where the prescription is made up?'

'At Raynham's, the chemist on the village high street. It is a very reputable establishment.' Lady Gayle tried to swallow, but her mouth was as dry as the Gobi Desert.

'Does the chemist make up the prescriptions on site?'

'Yes, I believe so.'

'And who owns the building?

'The building, Inspector, I'm sorry I don't understand. Which building are you talking about?'

'The building where these prescriptions are made up. The chemist's shop. Does Mr Raynham own the freehold, or is he a tenant?'

'I believe he is a tenant of the estate, Inspector.'

Inspector Coward thumbed a few pages of his notebook. 'And is the chemist up to date with his rent?'

'I couldn't tell you, Inspector.' Lady Gayle blinked, shaking her head slightly. 'Not off the top of my head. Mr Howden, my land agent, might have a better idea.'

'Oh, he does, my lady. Mr Howden was very helpful. Mr Raynham had been falling behind with his rent. The situation had been going on for some considerable time. But suddenly, the debt was paid in full. In fact, Mr Raynham has been able to make an advance payment on his rent. For the next two years. Can you explain that, my lady?'

'I cannot, Inspector. I don't think I like your insinuations. Do you have grounds to arrest me?'

'Not at the moment, my lady.' Inspector Coward bowed.

Lady Gayle glowered at him. *Is he mocking me?*

'Gayle, don't say another word.' Evelyn rose from her chair in the corner of the room where she'd placed herself to give the patient some breathing space. It clattered against the wall. 'Inspector, unless you have plans to arrest her ladyship, may I suggest that we continue this conversation at another time? Perhaps when her ladyship can have her solicitor present.'

Inspector Coward flushed. 'As you wish,' he said. He nodded to the women and left the room.

'Oh, Evelyn, you see what I mean. He's never been quite so horrid before, but I don't trust him. He is far too close to Colonel Gosforth.'

'Don't worry about him. I think we should get you back

to Bethencourt Castle and talk with your solicitor,' replied Evelyn, patting Lady Gayle's hand.

'And you'll come with me. You'll stay and help me?'

'Just try stopping me,' replied Evelyn Trent. 'I only need to place a few things in a case, and I can join you straightaway.'

'Oh, thank you, Evelyn. It will feel good to have someone on my side.'

CHAPTER TWENTY

It wasn't until the following day that Lady Gayle was able to leave the hospital and return to Bethencourt Castle with Evelyn. She ignored the opinions of Sister Edwards and the hospital doctor.

Only once she had settled into the first-class train carriage with Evelyn did she finally relax. She sat back in her seat with the window blind down as the train rushed her home.

'I finally feel safe,' said Lady Gayle. 'Thank you for coming home with me. Hopefully, no one else will try to shoot me.'

'Not even your neighbour, the colonel?'

'Even him. I know he wants to claim the piece of land back, but I can see it was won fair and square. He is owed nothing.'

'And there is no ghost prowling around in the attics?'

'Definitely not,' Lady Gayle replied with a shake of her head. 'The ghost is simply a tale. There's no truth in it. There are sometimes odd noises, but it's an old house. I'm so glad you are coming to stay with me. My life can finally return to normal.' She leaned against the headrest, closing her eyes, and trying to ignore the pain pulsating in her left arm where the stitches pulled the wound together. Then she remembered she hadn't asked the housekeeper about the food she'd found in the attic. *I must do that when I get home.*

However, Lady Gayle was exhausted when she arrived home, and the cheese-loving ghost was forgotten again. Evelyn insisted that she rested, and so she took to her room once she had asked Fredericks to arrange accommodation for Miss Trent.

Despite her protests that she felt perfectly well, Lady Gayle was confined to her room for the next few days, but the enforced rest was more than she could cope with, and she was anxious for some escape from the four walls of her bedroom.

'We'll go for a ride around the estate, Evelyn,' Lady Gayle said. 'I feel like a prisoner here, and my arm is much better.'

'If you are sure, Gayle,' said Evelyn. 'I think you should listen to the doctor and rest a little longer. You could open the stitches.'

'No, we'll take it easy; I can ride one-handed.' And so it was decided, and the following morning, the two ladies headed for the stables. Lady Gayle wore her new breeches, and Evelyn was using her old riding habit. The habit worn by Lady Sylvia had been cleaned and put back in the attic. Alice had tried to repair the hole, but it was far too large. Throwing the garment away may have been a more sensible idea, but nothing was ever wasted.

When they walked into the stable yard, Shepherd had

the horses ready. Evelyn was given old Bessie, but she was still rather nervous.

'You don't have to be so scared. Relax your hands; otherwise, you'll take her teeth out,' Lady Gayle called to Evelyn.

'I can't help it. I'm not used to horses. I was brought up in a town, you know,' replied Evelyn.

'Bessie will take care of you. She's as gentle as a lamb.' Lady Gayle glanced back at her friend with a frown. 'Relax, come along, you'll be fine. You used to ride all the time when we were in France.'

'That doesn't mean I enjoyed it,' muttered Evelyn. She settled into the saddle, however, and they rode out of the yard; the faces of both rider and horse were ones of long-suffering. As the party neared the woods on the border between Bethencourt Castle land and that owned by Colonel Gosforth, a gunshot rang out.

Evelyn's face blanched. She gripped the reins tightly, and Bessie, annoyed by this latest insult, grasped the bit between her teeth and put her head down. She bucked once, and Evelyn was on the ground. Lady Gayle wanted to laugh, but one look at Evelyn's furious face quelled her mirth. Bessie, having rid herself of her rider, wandered to the fence and began to munch on the grass. Evelyn rose, brushed herself down and quickly captured the mare.

Then another shot rang out. Much nearer than the first one, and Plantagenet danced nervously on the spot; Lady Gayle patted his neck to calm him. Just as she had him under control once more, Colonel Gosforth burst from the hedgerow brandishing a shotgun.

'I might have known it was you making all the noise. You've frightened the birds off. I'll get no more sport this afternoon,' the colonel shouted. His puce face was puffed up, and he was waving the gun around dangerously.

'Please stop waving your shotgun around, Colonel,' said Lady Gayle. She still stroked Plantagenet's neck with her injured left arm, holding him on a tight rein with her right hand to stop him shaking his head. 'You're scaring our horses.' She glanced at Evelyn to ensure she was all right. Evelyn still had hold of Bessie and was stroking her nose. They both appeared to be fine.

The colonel glared at her, but all the same, he pressed his thumb against the top lever, opening the gun and ejecting two cartridges. He held the open gun in the crook of his right elbow.

Lady Gayle stared from the two cartridge cases on the ground to the colonel, and reluctantly, he bent down to retrieve them.

'I thought you were still in London,' he muttered.

'Is that why you saw fit to trespass on my land?'

'Nonsense, girl. I was on my own land where I can do what I like.'

'Well, you are not on your own land now, Colonel. You are on my land, and I'd be grateful if you would leave it.' Lady Gayle glared at him, breathing deeply. The sound of racing blood pounded through her ears.

'I did hear someone took a potshot at you though.' A grin took over from the normal sneer on the colonel's face.

'They were a bad shot. They missed,' replied Lady Gayle. She touched the spot on her neck where the wound was healing. The colonel didn't need to know the truth. 'It wasn't you by any chance?'

'I wouldn't have missed,' snarled the colonel. 'I was a crack shot in my younger days. You'd be six feet under if I'd taken a shot at you.'

'Thank you, Colonel, however, these are not your younger days, are they?' retorted Lady Gayle. She edged Plantagenet closer to the colonel. 'I will be happy to let the police know that you've just made a threat to my life.'

'I did nothing of the sort, young lady. I merely reassured you that if it had been me, I would not have missed. I know that my life would be much improved without you in it.'

'That's a horrible thing to say,' shouted Evelyn. She ran at the colonel, riding crop raised in her left hand and dragging poor Bessie behind her.

'Oh crikey,' Lady Gayle shouted. She swung her right leg over the saddle and slipped to the ground. 'Evelyn, don't. He's not worth it.'

Evelyn dropped her hand and whirled around to face Lady Gayle. 'It was a horrid thing to say,' she repeated.

'It was, but I don't think a horsewhipping will improve his manners. Let's go back to the castle.' She turned to the colonel. 'Colonel, please leave and do not let me catch you on my land again. You are not welcome.'

'No, I'm not going to let him ruin our ride. Get me back on this beast, and we'll carry on with seeing your lands.' Evelyn gathered Bessie's reins in one hand and faced the saddle.

Lady Gayle gave her a one-handed boost, biting her lips with pain. Once she saw her friend was settled in Bessie's saddle, she used the wooden fence to regain her own seat. She nodded to Evelyn, and they headed off. As the path narrowed and they neared the spot where Lady Sylvia had fallen, Evelyn halted Bessie and stared down the slope.

'You'll be fine,' called Lady Gayle, twisting around in her saddle to look back. She noticed her friend's pale face and wondered if one of the servants had told Evelyn that this was the spot. 'Look straight ahead and not down the slope. Trust Bessie. She won't take you down there.'

Evelyn gave her a faint smile, but it seemed as if she were unable to draw her eyes away from the slope and the rushing brook below.

'How long was she down there?' she said finally.

Lady Gayle backed Plantagenet until he was alongside Bessie. Despite his agility, the grey was still a large horse, and the path was not wide enough to turn him around.

'She was down there for hours,' she said. 'Absolutely ages. It must have been dreadfully frightening.'

'Yes, I suppose it must have been. And now the inspector thinks that the bullet was intended for you?'

'I'm not sure what the inspector thinks anymore, but you heard our conversation at the hospital. I think he suspected me of trying to kill Lady Sylvia and my father. However, since the attempt in London, I suppose it's more likely that I was the target—'

'But you escaped again. You must have as many lives as a cat.' Evelyn pursed her lips, turning away from the view down the slope.

Lady Gayle laughed. 'I suppose I must. You look pale, Evelyn. Perhaps we should go back now. I don't want you catching a chill. I'm sure the inspector would frown upon my having a sick house guest.'

Evelyn rubbed her arms. 'I am rather cold,' she said. 'I think a nice warm fire would be very welcome.'

CHAPTER TWENTY-ONE

STILL CHATTERING FROM THE COLD OF THE EARLY DECEMBER DAY, Lady Gayle and Evelyn burst into the drawing room and bore down upon the fire.

'Have you called for tea, Mama?' said Lady Gayle. 'I'm ravenous, aren't you, Evelyn?'

'Yes, definitely. Very hungry. Nothing like going into battle to raise your appetite.'

'Battle?' The Dowager Countess glanced at her daughter with a raised eyebrow. 'Pray tell, who have you been taking to task?'

'Colonel Gosforth,' came the reply. 'I found him trespassing on my land, and I told him to leave.' Lady Gayle glanced at Evelyn as she giggled.

'It sounds like there was more to it than that,' replied her mother. 'Evelyn, my dear, perhaps I can prevail upon you to tell me the truth of the matter.'

Evelyn flushed. 'The colonel did not behave like a gentleman, and we asked him to leave castle grounds.'

'That doesn't sound like much of a battle,' said the

Dowager Countess. She seemed about to say more but broke off as the door opened, and Fredericks brought in a tray of tea and sandwiches. 'Thank you, Fredericks,' she said, and the butler bowed and left the room.

Silence commenced as the three women drank tea and ate the variety of delicacies on offer.

'I forgot to mention, Gayle, while you were out, Fredericks wanted a quiet chat.'

'Is there a problem, Mama?'

'It seems our ghost is up to his old tricks.'

'A ghost?' said Evelyn. 'You really have a ghost?'

'It's all stuff and nonsense,' replied Lady Ethel. 'But it seems to have upset the maids, especially Miss Smith.'

'Miss Smith? Do you mean Sarah?' asked Lady Gayle.

'Yes, Smith is her name now. I refuse to call her Snodgrass,' said her mother. 'She doesn't seem to be working out after all. I thought she would be a suitable lady's maid, but we'll have to let her go.'

Lady Gayle glanced at Evelyn. It wasn't appropriate to talk about such matters in front of a guest, but Evelyn was such a very old friend. 'Perhaps we could discuss this later, Mama? I don't believe she had been with Lady Sylvia for very long. I understand Sylvia was unhappy with her too.'

'You could have mentioned this before. I feel very affronted that you offered me a substandard maid.'

'Mama, every maid you have ever had has been considered substandard. Lady Sylvia thought she could improve the girl. Evelyn, how do you find her services? Is Sarah satisfactory?'

'I have scarcely needed her. Of course, I'm really not used to having a maid, but she keeps everything nice and seems to know what I'll want before I do. I have no complaints, but I have hardly required her help.' Evelyn's cheeks were pink, and she appeared embarrassed by the conversation.

'She sounds like quite a paragon,' said Lady Gayle. 'Let's give her a few more weeks, Mama, and see how she gets on. I'd hate to dismiss her now so close to Christmas.'

'You should not be so sentimental about domestic staff, Gayle. They will take advantage,' announced the Dowager Countess.

Feeling warmth flood her face, Lady Gayle dipped her head. 'Yes, Mama,' she said. She raised her teacup to sip more tea but found her hands shaking with anger. 'Mama, perhaps we could have this conversation later. We do need to discuss the staff in more detail, but it's all rather boring for Evelyn.' She set the teacup on a side table, rose, and strolled to the windows, staring out into the darkness. She clenched and unclenched her fists while she considered her new role. They had not had more than a few staff before moving to Bethencourt Castle. Now, with inside and outside staff, it felt as if she had a small army to oversee.

Will I ever become used to this life? Do I even want to?

After tea, Lady Gayle retired to her room to bathe and change from her riding breeches. She had some letters to attend to before dinner.

Alice was laying out an afternoon dress when she walked into the room.

'Thank you, Alice,' she said. 'I think I shall want a shawl this evening. It was very cold outside this afternoon.'

'Yes, milady.' Alice bobbed, but she didn't return to her work and stood twisting her fingers.

'Is there something wrong, Alice?'

'I don't want to speak out of turn, milady.'

'However, you do wish to speak about something?'

Alice nodded rapidly, wiping her eyes with the corner of her white apron.

'You had better sit down,' said Lady Gayle. She directed Alice to one of the armchairs by the fire. Using tongs, she placed a few lumps of coal on the fire, dismissing Alice's concerns that she should be stoking up the fire and not her mistress.

She waited for Alice to begin talking, but the maid sat mutely. 'Perhaps you could tell me what this is all about? Has someone upset you?'

Alice nodded, hanging her head, and twisting a corner of her apron. 'It's that Sarah Snodgrass' she said eventually. 'She's been teasing me about the ghost.'

'I see. Tell me, what's been happening?'

Alice nodded again. 'She came up to the attics with me to look for a riding habit for Miss Evelyn and... well, she kept telling me stories and trying to scare me. Then, when we were about to come down again, she said she was going to lock me in the attic. Oh, milady, you know how it gets so dark in there. I have to say I was a little afraid. Sarah kept making ghost noises and calling me a coward and a simpleton.'

Lady Gayle drew her bottom lip in under her teeth. Perhaps, even with Christmas looming, it would be best to let Sarah go after all. 'Have you spoken with Mr Fredericks?'

'Oh no, milady. I spoke to Mrs Mitchell, and she said she would deal with it.'

Lady Gayle nodded, rose, and rang the bell. Fredericks rapidly appeared. 'Fredericks, would you be so kind as to ask Mrs Mitchell to join me in the library? I have a matter to discuss with her.'

'Very good, my lady,' replied the butler. He gave a half-bow as he left.

Mrs Mitchell was on her knees in the process of lighting the newly laid fire in the library when Lady Gayle entered the room.

The older woman scrambled to her feet, dropping into a curtsy. 'I'm sorry, my lady, the fire was allowed to go out in this room. It won't happen again.'

'That's not quite what I wanted to talk to you about, Mrs Mitchell. But it is related.' Lady Gayle seated herself on the sofa closest to the newly lit fire. 'Tell me, who was responsible for seeing to the fire in this room?'

'It's normally a job for one of the parlour maids, my lady. There's only Jenny and Katie now, and it's their afternoon off today. We had more maids before the war, but...' Mrs Mitchell twisted her hands in her lap. 'To be honest, my lady, I don't know how much longer they will stay.'

'Oh dear,' said Lady Gayle. 'That is going to be a nuisance. Are there any girls in the village looking for good, honest work?'

'I don't think so, my lady. Although I keep my ear to the ground. Girls don't want to work in service anymore, and they don't want to be stuck out in the country. There are many, much more exciting opportunities in town. They can earn more money, and of course, they meet young men.' Mrs Mitchell sniffed with disapproval.

Lady Gayle nodded. 'I quite understand,' she said. 'It was about one of the maids I wanted to have a chat about. Sarah. Lady Sylvia's lady's maid.'

'Oh yes, my lady.' Mrs Mitchell sat up straight, drawing her lips into a thin line. 'She's not satisfactory. Not at all.'

'I understand there was an upset earlier in the attics?'

'She threatened to lock Alice in, really upset her, she did. Alice isn't one to scare easily, as you know, but that Sarah has a way of getting under your skin. If you'll pardon me being so frank, does your ladyship plan to keep her on?'

'I haven't decided. It's why I wanted to speak with you. I've had no dealings with the girl. However, it's very upsetting that she cannot maintain a cordial relationship with Alice. How does she get on with the other staff?'

'She's sly, my lady.' Mrs Mitchell sniffed. 'Says one thing and does another.'

'I see, well, Miss Evelyn seems to find her work satisfactory, so, I suggest we keep her while Miss Evelyn is with us and then reassess the situation.'

A cloud passed over Mrs Mitchell's face, and then it was gone. 'As you wish, my lady.' She rose and glanced at the fire. 'Will you issue an order for the attics to be locked, my lady?'

'I will think about it,' said Lady Gayle. 'I don't suppose you know anything about food being left in the attics, do you? Bread. Cheese. That sort of thing.'

'No, my lady. I haven't heard anything like that. Perhaps that would be another good reason for locking the attic rooms. If the staff can't get in there, then there will be less trouble.'

'Do the staff go up there often? I cannot see that there would be any need.'

'You'd think not, my lady, but whenever that Sarah is missing, you can rest assured that that's where she can be found.'

'Does she have an explanation?'

'No, my lady. She denies going up there, but where else would she get cobwebs or dust on her uniform?'

Lady Gayle nodded. 'Where indeed,' she said. *This is very puzzling. Very puzzling indeed.*

CHAPTER
TWENTY-TWO

THE FOLLOWING DAY, HAVING ASSURED HERSELF THAT EVELYN WAS happily occupied and not feeling ignored, Lady Gayle resumed her duties as the new landlord and went to meet more of her tenants. The land agent, Mr Howden, returned but refused to ride Seamus again. Poor Bessie was once more given the task of carrying him, which clearly put tremendous strain on the elderly mare.

Lady Gayle glared at him as Bessie struggled to carry him out of the stable yard. She sighed, folding her arms. *Perhaps it is time to retire all the horses and use motor vehicles instead, but I am not going to destroy a healthy horse, whatever Mr Howden says.* She came to a decision. 'Shepherd, could you ask around and see if we can find a replacement for Bessie.'

Shepherd removed his flat cap and twisted it in his hands. 'I can but ask, my lady,' he said. 'Not many of the horses that were taken for the war were ever returned.'

'I know it's likely to be a thankless task, Shepherd,' she replied. 'All the same, I'd like to do it for Bessie's sake. She should be retired, poor old girl.'

'Right, you are, my lady.' Shepherd smoothed his hair and replaced his cap. 'I'll see what I can do.'

'Thank you, Shepherd. I'll ask all the neighbours too. There must be someone with a horse suitable to carry Mr Howden.'

Lady Gayle stared after the land agent and the poor mare. She decided. 'Mr Howden,' she called. 'I've changed my mind. I have a desire to see the brewery this morning. Come back, and Chadwick will take us in the car.'

Relief suffused Howden's face. He halted Bessie and turned her around. Sensing a return to her box, Bessie began to trot, and the land agent slipped around on her back, looking for all the world like a badly tied parcel which was coming undone.

'We could go in my car,' he said. 'It's just there.'

Trying to maintain an impassive visage, Lady Gayle turned her gaze to the small black vehicle, which was leaking oil on her stable yard once again. At least horses have never leaked oil everywhere, she thought, nibbling her lip. 'We could do that, Mr Howden, if you think your car will be up to the journey. You really must do something about that leak, you know,' she replied slowly. 'I would also like to change my clothes, and I will need to return to the house to do that.'

Howden's face took on a glum expression. 'It's been repaired a few times,' he said, slipping from Bessie's back. He dropped to his knees to look under the car. 'But nothing seems to fix it.' He rose and scratched his head.

Lady Gayle frowned down at him. 'A leaky engine really doesn't lend strength to your argument that motor vehicles are better for getting around the estate, does it?'

'No, my lady, it does not. I will endeavour to get it repaired again.'

'Very well,' she said. 'We'll go in your car, but only after I have changed out of these breeches.'

'Splendid,' he said, his face split by his huge smile. He slapped his pockets, holding up the car key as a sort of prize. He opened the passenger side door for her.

Lady Gayle's eyes widened. She slipped from Plantagenet's saddle and handed the reins to Shepherd, trying hard to ignore the head groom's grin. She glanced at him, and the smile disappeared instantly. As she walked towards Mr Howden's car, she resisted the temptation to look back. She was convinced the head groom was still smiling at her discomfort.

Mr Howden held open the passenger door for her, and Lady Gayle seated herself, wriggling to get comfortable in the cramped space.

'It's very kind of you to offer to drive, but I could have walked back to the house,' she said. 'I won't take long to change.'

'Take as long as you need, your ladyship.' Mr Howden shut the door and strolled to the other side of the vehicle. He rested his hands on the steering wheel for a moment. 'It's not quite like the Bentley,' he said, glancing at her. 'But I was very pleased when his lordship gave me this car.'

'My father?'

'No, my lady. Lord Percival. He was always very generous to me.' Howden started the engine, and the small Austin rattled into life.

Lady Gayle clutched her seat. *Why was Great Uncle Percival so generous?* She peeked at Mr Howden, but he was squinting ahead, pushing his thick glasses into place. His expression gave nothing away.

'Were you here with my uncle during the war?' She tried to make the question appear innocuous but noticed the sharp glance he gave her.

'I wasn't fit to serve, my lady,' he muttered. 'I wanted to do my bit, of course I did, but I had rheumatic fever as a child, so I have a dicky ticker. Plus, the old eyesight isn't top-notch, as you've probably noticed.'

Lady Gayle nodded. Both her cousins had joined the regulars as soon as war was declared. Maxwell had joined from Oxford University and Rupert straight from school. Neither had survived the first year. If they had, she wouldn't be sitting here now.

'Lord Percival wasn't like other landlords; he was good to his tenants,' continued Mr Howden. 'Sir Vernon Thackery over at Plumstead Manor forced all his servants and tenants to join up. Said they wouldn't have jobs to return to if they didn't fight. Lord Percival encouraged people to join up, of course he did, and he promised to pay half wages to the families until the men returned. But he never threatened. He was a good master.'

'You must have admired him greatly,' said Lady Gayle.

Mr Howden sniffed and removed his glasses. He wiped his eyes with the back of his hand, and Lady Gayle looked out of the window, pretending not to notice. She hadn't realised the land agent and her uncle had been so close.

Lady Gayle let herself out of the Austin when he parked the car at the foot of the castle steps. She ran to her room, changed quickly, and dashed downstairs again. As she reached the hall, Mr Howden was standing staring at the portrait of Lord Percival. There was a strange smile playing around his lips. He hadn't noticed her, and she watched him for a moment and smiled to herself. *Of course, in the right light, he does have a look of Maxwell about him. No wonder the old man became so fond of Mr Howden. Perhaps I could ask Fredericks later if there's anything else I need to know.*

They drove through the village and out the other side. Near the river, there was a large brick building with several steaming chimneys. Bethencourt Brewery, she read on the sign as they drove through the large wooden gates.

As the car drew to a halt, a short, tubby man snatched open the passenger side door. Deep brown eyes shone in a ruddy face.

'I'm so pleased to meet you, Countess Bethencourt,' he said. 'I'm Ted Bennett, Master Brewer and manager here. Welcome to Bethencourt Brewery.'

Lady Gayle swung her legs out of the car and stood. She desperately wanted to stretch but heard her mother's voice making remarks about being unseemly. Instead, she nodded her head, shook the proffered hand, and followed the little man into the building.

Once inside, she unbuttoned her coat; there was no way she would survive this heat in a thick winter coat.

'It's quite a contrast to outside, isn't it, my lady?' Mr Bennett beamed at her. The smile caused his face to round until he resembled a ball with eyes. It was most disarming.

'It most certainly is,' she replied. 'What must it be like in the summer?'

'Even hotter,' came the reply. 'You may leave your coat in my office, if you wish, my lady.' Mr Bennett held his hand out, but she shook her head and laid it over her arm, confident she could manage to carry it for the tour of the works.

It was much warmer inside the brewery rooms. The large wooden tuns used to brew the beer were hot to the touch. As they passed by one which was uncovered, Lady

Gayle peeked over the edge. To her surprise, the brewer grasped her arm and pulled her back.

'Careful, my lady,' he said. 'There are still poisonous gases in there. We leave the tuns open so the gas can disperse before someone goes in and cleans it all out.'

'Isn't that dangerous?' Lady Gayle still wanted to stare over the edge and see inside the large barrel.

'It's very dangerous indeed, my lady. We take every precaution we can, and we've not lost anyone at this brewery.'

'That's good news,' replied Lady Gayle.

The tour took some considerable time, more than Lady Gayle had expected, and it was lunchtime by the time they were back at the head brewer's office.

Fredericks had arrived with a basket and luncheon prepared by the cook. Mr Howden and Mr Bennett tucked in, but her ladyship's appetite had been quelled by the heat.

'How many men do you employ here, Mr Bennett,' she asked, sipping some of the lemonade which had been brought from her kitchen.

'Not as many as before the war, my lady,' replied the brewer. 'We're building up again with boys who were too young to fight but are starting work now. We'll be back to full production in two years by my reckoning.'

Lady Gayle nodded. The Bethencourt Arms was currently taking beer from other breweries, she knew. Once the Bethencourt Brewery could supply its own public house and to others, then the tide of monies would be inwards rather than flowing away from the estate.

She resumed her lunch, mulling over the prosperity of the Bethencourt estate.

CHAPTER TWENTY-THREE

Lady Gayle drank the early morning coffee that Alice brought for her.

'What are your plans for today, milady?'

'I want to go and meet Mr Raynham, the chemist. Then I'd like to find out who sent the roses. I know they arrived on the milk train, so they must have been sent from London, but why and who were they for?'

'It sounds like you are going to carry on with your investigations, milady?'

'Yes, Alice. I am. I've allowed myself to become distracted with the estate, but some strange things happened that I would like to get to the bottom of.'

'Very good, milady. Is Miss Trent or Mr Howden going with you to the chemist?'

'I think I am going on my own. Miss Trent said she has some letters to write. Perhaps you could accompany me?' Lady Gayle replied. 'I believe Mr Howden is going to the livestock market with Mr Shepherd today. He suggested we improve the dairy herd. And hopefully, they will be able to find a replacement for poor Bessie.'

'If Mr Howden is choosing the horse, it will be the quietest one there.'

Lady Gayle laughed. 'Yes, he does seem quite terrified. He must find something that can carry him though. Bessie's not tall enough, and she should have been put out to grass long ago.'

Lady Gayle pushed back her bedclothes. 'Has my mother gone down to breakfast, do you know?'

'No, milady. Sarah said the Dowager Countess was having breakfast in her room. Not well enough to go downstairs.'

'I didn't know Mama was unwell. I shall see her after breakfast. Am I in black again?' Lady Gayle bent to look in the mirror, pinching her cheeks to add some colour.

'Yes, milady, although I did see in *Vogue* magazine this summer that you can wear a little jewellery if you choose. A single string of pearls or perhaps that black onyx necklace.'

'Very well,' sighed Lady Gayle. 'I barely seemed to be out of mourning for Hugh when I had to start again for Uncle Percival and then for my father. Still, it can't be helped, and there are so many ladies in the same situation.'

'It won't be long until spring, milady. You'll be in half-mourning then.'

'That's something to look forward to,' said Lady Gayle. She drew her thick cardigan around her slim body and made for the door. Barely had she reached it than Alice was there opening it for her. Nodding her thanks, she made her way downstairs, wondering if she could beat Fredericks to the dining room door. It was a silly game, but it kept her amused.

Yet again, it was a game she was destined to lose.

. . .

After her breakfast, Lady Gayle went to her mother's room. 'Good morning, Mama,' she said. 'I was told you are unwell. I am going into the village this morning. May I collect anything for you?'

'Sarah has called Dr Sloane. He should be here directly. I simply have one of my heads.'

'Perhaps you should drink more water, Mama? Dehydration can cause headaches. I learned that during the war.'

Her mother snorted and pushed away the magazine she had been reading. 'More of your new-fangled nonsense,' she said. 'I'll wait to see what a qualified medical man has to say, if you don't mind. Why are you going into the village? You have no reason to go there.'

'I want to meet the chemist, Mama. He's one of our tenants. I haven't met him yet.'

'So long as you're not doing more of your detecting. That's not at all appropriate for a young lady.'

'You were quite happy for me to clear my name not so very long ago, Mama. Do I need remind you?'

Her mother gave a haughty sniff. 'You should be seeking out a new husband. I see you've already abandoned mourning for your poor Papa.'

'Not in the slightest, Mama. I'm wearing black, although I have decided against the crepe.'

'You are wearing jewellery!'

'Just a string of black beads. It helps cover the mark on my neck.'

'This is where all your detecting gets you. People take potshots.'

'Yes, Mama, there could be no other reason.' Lady Gayle noticed the maid Sarah loitering in the doorway to her mother's dressing room. For a moment, she was annoyed with herself for letting the woman know she was visiting the chemist but then dismissed the idea. Sarah could not have poisoned her father as she was in London with Lady Sylvia at the time.

Once outside her mother's room, she shook her head. You're seeing killers everywhere, she told herself.

Lady Gayle returned to her room and, once attired for the chill autumn day, lady and maid set out to walk to the village.

'Are you recovered from your fright yesterday, Alice?'

'Yes, milady. I think so.'

'Mrs Mitchell says Sarah spends a lot of time in the attics. Have you seen her up there many times?'

'Well, I couldn't say, milady.' Alice tucked her chin against her chest—her face hidden by the brim of her bonnet.

'Alice, can't say or won't? What *aren't* you telling me?'

'Well, milady, I don't like to tell tales out of school...'

'But?'

'But it's not just Sarah, milady. Miss Evelyn spends a lot of time in the attics too. I think they are looking for something.'

'I see.' Lady Gayle frowned. What on earth could her friend be looking for in the attics? 'What does Mrs Mitchell say?'

'I haven't said anything to Mrs Mitchell,' replied Alice.

'I see. I shall speak with Miss Evelyn when we return to the castle. Tell me, is it my imagination, or is everyone staring at me?'

'It's not your imagination, milady. I've noticed it myself. There's been talk about too many deaths at the castle. Mr

Fredericks says the villagers think that someone must be to blame.'

'And that somebody has to be me?'

'I really couldn't say, milady,' Alice replied with her head dipped.

As they opened the door to the chemist's shop, a bell clattered loudly, announcing their arrival. A pretty young woman with shiny dark hair bobbed in the latest fashion appeared. Her face blanched when she saw who the customers were.

Flustered, she dropped into a half curtsy. 'Good morning, your ladyship,' she said. 'How may I help you?'

'Is Mr Raynham available? I would like to consult with him,' said Lady Gayle.

The girl, for she was hardly more than fifteen, gaped, her mouth opening and closing like a landed trout.

Beside her, Lady Gayle felt Alice's elbow quiver. She dared not look at her maid for fear of being overcome with the same urge to laugh at the girl's shock. 'Well?' she said, using the deep tone her mother used when annoyed.

The half curtsy was repeated, and the girl dashed behind the curtain. Hurried voices were heard, and a man in a white doctor's style coat appeared. He bowed his head. 'To what do I owe this pleasure, your ladyship?'

Lady Gayle stared at the brilliantine, slicking back his hair with horror. The oil had marked the top of his collar, producing a grey, slimy-looking edging. She shuddered but gathered her wits. 'Lord Cedric, my late father,' she began. 'His heart powders, were they prepared here by you?'

'Normally, I would prepare all medicines and powders

here, but those were ones Dr Sloane ordered from London. May I ask the sudden interest?'

'Sudden?' repeated Lady Gayle.

'The Scotland Yard detective was here asking the same questions only a few days ago. He took some samples of the powders with him.'

Lady Gayle and Alice exchanged a glance. 'Perhaps you could furnish me with the name of the London supplier?'

Mr Raynham bowed again. His hair was so thickly coated with hair oil it didn't move. 'Of course, my lady,' he said, and with a flourish, he picked up a notepad. He wrote the name down and held the slip of paper out towards her ladyship.

Alice reached forward and took it from his grasp before handing the paper to her mistress. Lady Gayle placed it straight in her handbag, nodded and left the shop.

They made their way across the high street to the tea shop where, once again, Lady Gayle's presence caused consternation, but they were soon seated at a window seat some distance away from the few other customers, with a pot of tea and delicious-looking cakes.

'I did wonder if Mr Raynham had put additional digitalis in my father's heart powders,' Lady Gayle mused as she sipped the tea Alice had poured for her. She kept her voice low, looking around to ensure no one was listening.

'If he didn't, though, doesn't that mean that the poison was added in London?' said Alice in a whisper.

'Either that or by someone in the house,' replied Lady Gayle. 'I know which option I prefer. I can't bear to think that anyone at Bethencourt Castle would have a hand in murdering my father.'

'I can't believe anyone at the castle would have hurt your father, milady. But that only leaves us two options, doesn't it?'

Lady Gayle nodded in agreement. 'The poison was either added by Mr Raynham, or it was added beforehand in London.'

'Didn't you say that Mr Raynham had recently come into money, milady?'

'Yes, according to Mr Howden, he's gone from being behind with his rent to being well ahead. Unfortunately for Mr Raynham, as far as I can see, that can only mean that someone has paid him for something nefarious.'

CHAPTER TWENTY-FOUR

After finishing their tea and cakes, Lady Gayle and Alice strolled to the railway station.

The stationmaster had no recollection of the roses arriving, and disappointed, Lady Gayle and Alice began to retrace their steps to Bethencourt Castle.

'Milady, milady.'

The shouts came from a stout woman of middle years who was waving a red accounts book similar to the ones that Mr Howden liked to drag her through despite her lack of interest. Lady Gayle's heart sank. Not more accounts, she thought.

'Thank you for stopping, milady.' The woman bent over, panting loudly. 'I'm the stationmaster's wife. I keep a note of all arrivals in case there's a problem later. If you would be so kind as to come back to my parlour, I can show you.'

Lady Gayle raised her eyebrows but acquiesced. She and Alice followed the woman back to the station. At the side of the main building was a squat cottage with evergreen shrubs in baskets.

'That's all the colour we can get at this time of year,' the woman offered as an explanation. 'I do like a bit of colour around the place, don't you, milady?'

Lady Gayle gave a brief smile, 'I do, Mrs...'

'Barns, milady. Tilly Barns. Do come in.'

Mrs Barns opened the front door, and a maid of all works scampered towards them. 'Tea, Dotty,' said Mrs Barns, 'bring us some tea.'

'Please, Mrs Barns, do not trouble yourself, my maid and I have just taken tea at the tea shop. I simply couldn't manage another sip.'

Disappointment wafted across Mrs Barns' face, and she waved her maid away before showing Lady Gayle and Alice into her parlour.

There was a roaring fire in the hearth, blasting heat into the room. Lady Gayle loosened her scarf and sat in a chair near the window where it was cooler.

Mrs Barns opened her accounts book and turned it so Lady Gayle could see the entries. There it was, 16th November 1922, one bouquet of pink roses for immediate delivery to Bethencourt Castle.

Written in Mrs Barns' copperplate hand were the words "No card. Florist, Cracknell's of Bond Street".

Lady Gayle clapped her hands with glee. 'That's marvellous,' she said. 'I can telegram Cracknell's and ask them who ordered the flowers.'

Rising from her chair and making ready to leave, Lady Gayle turned, resting her gloved hand on the polished doorknob. 'Thank you, Mrs Barns, your thoroughness has saved me a great deal of trouble.'

Lady Gayle hurried back towards Bethencourt Castle with Alice scurrying along behind her.

'Milady, please could you slow down?' Alice puffed.

'I'm sorry, Alice, but I think I've solved it,' replied Lady Gayle. 'I think I know who sent the flowers and why.'

'Milady?' Alice halted and clung to a gate to get her breath back.

'I was beginning to wonder if Mr Howden was behind everything.' Lady Gayle looked back at her maid and drew to a halt.

'Are you sure, milady?' Alice's face was clouded in confusion.

'Come along, Alice, there isn't a moment to lose. He must be in league with Sarah Snodgrass. She's been his spy here. I saw her staring at the portraits recently, and then, before we went to the brewery, I saw Mr Howden looking at the portraits too. I do think that Mr Howden looks remarkably like my cousin Maxwell.'

'Does he, milady? I did hear tell the other day that the car Mr Howden has been given previously belonged to Mr Maxwell.'

'It did?' gasped Lady Gayle. 'Gosh, he told me that Lord Percival gave him the car. He didn't say why.' Her mind raced. *Does that mean Harold Howden was born on the wrong side of the blanket, and his father was none other than Lord Percival?* 'We must send this telegram to Cracknell's urgently.'

'What about the post office, milady? Can we send it from there, and then we don't need to run all the way back to the castle?'

'Splendid idea, Alice.' Lady Gayle rushed across the road to the post office, and Alice ran behind her as quickly as she could.

Once in the post office, the telegram was duly composed and sent. Lady Gayle hesitated a moment and sent another to the London chemist who'd made up her father's heart powders. Alice wandered around the small shop that was attached to the post office, occasionally gazing out of the window. Once Lady Gayle had completed her tasks, she and her maid returned to the castle at a more sedate pace.

When they arrived back at Bethencourt Castle, Fredericks appeared very flustered. At first, Lady Gayle thought that it was because Alice had accompanied her through the front door. Before she could ask him, however, her mother dashed into the hallway.

'Where have you been?' she said. 'There's terrible news. Colonel Gosforth has been badly injured. It seems the stupid man had an accident with his shotgun.'

'An accident?' replied Lady Gayle. 'How can one have an accident with a shotgun? Has he shot himself?'

Her mother nodded, fanning herself with one of her black lace-trimmed handkerchiefs. 'That's what we've been told,' she said.

'But how? Do you want to go and see Mrs Gosforth, Mama?' said Lady Gayle. She rubbed her forehead. 'Are you sure it was an accident? Even the colonel isn't that foolish.'

'I think I'd like to see Mrs Gosforth; she sent only the briefest of notes,' said the Dowager Countess. 'Will you come with me?'

On the point of refusing, since her recent encounters with the colonel had not been the most auspicious, Lady Gayle gave in. It was rare for her mother to be this distraught. 'Let me freshen up,' she said. She turned to the butler, who was hovering in the background. 'Fredericks, could you ask for the Bentley to be brought round? Mama, sit down for a moment. Everything is going to be just fine.'

She headed for the stairs and her room, wondering if

the colonel really had had an accident or if there was something more sinister afoot.

She changed swiftly and was soon in the Bentley with her mother and on the way to Lockington Court. Could the colonel have meant to shoot himself? A shotgun was not the most convenient of weapons to use. A pistol was much more practical. After a quick glance at her mother's countenance, she told herself that sharing these thoughts would be most inadvisable.

When the ladies arrived at the Gosforths' home, Dr Sloane was already with his patient. Ladies Ethel and Gayle retired to the drawing room to comfort Mrs Gosforth.

'Oh, my dear, such a to-do,' exclaimed Mrs Gosforth. The older ladies greeted each other, both waving handkerchiefs in the air. Lady Gayle made for the hallway and called a servant to fetch tea. Once the calming balm was being consumed, she felt able to ask some questions, but Mrs Gosforth was unable to answer any. She knew nothing other than her husband had been on the wrong end of his own shotgun.

When Dr Sloane appeared, he was unable to offer an explanation either. 'I've given the colonel a sedative,' he said. 'He'll sleep until the morning.'

Lady Gayle nodded, unsure that she could achieve anything while the colonel was unable to talk. 'Mama,' she said. 'I think I should return to Bethencourt. Will you stay with Mrs Gosforth?'

Her mother gave her a sharp-eyed glance but acquiesced. 'I'll stay with Mrs Gosforth tonight,' she said.

After agreeing to send her mother's lady's maid with overnight things, Lady Gayle returned home.

. . .

Once she arrived at Bethencourt Castle, Lady Gayle and Alice retired to her ladyship's rooms to discuss the recent events.

'The colonel will live,' said Lady Gayle. 'At least Dr Sloane was able to assure me of that.'

'If he wants to,' muttered Alice darkly.

Lady Gayle nodded. It was certainly something to take into consideration. 'I still need to speak to Evelyn,' said Lady Gayle, 'and ask her about what she's after in the attic. Could you find out where she is?'

'I asked Mr Fredericks to let me know. She was in the library earlier, milady. There's been no message to say she's moved.'

'Very well,' replied Lady Gayle. She strode out of the room and downstairs to the library. Evelyn, seated by the fire, was engrossed in a book she was holding close to her face and didn't look up.

'Evelyn,' said Lady Gayle, 'might I interrupt you for a moment?'

Evelyn raised her head, her expression seeming, at least to Lady Gayle, to indicate that she'd known her ladyship was there all along. She closed the book after turning down a corner to mark her place.

Lady Gayle swallowed before she spoke, noticing that the book was a first edition of *Jane Eyre*. 'Are you quite comfortable, my dear?' she began. 'I'm sorry that I've been busy recently. There's always such a lot to do with the estate. I am afraid I've been neglecting you.'

'I've found ways to occupy myself,' replied Evelyn. 'You have a marvellous library here, and I wanted to explore it.'

'I am glad you like it,' said Lady Gayle. 'Have you only explored the library? There are some fine paintings in the portrait gallery. I know your maid has enjoyed looking at them.'

'My maid? Oh, you mean Sarah. I didn't know she was interested in art.'

'Art and attics, it seems. And now it appears you, too, are interested in attics.'

'I don't follow,' said Evelyn. Then she glanced at the novel on her lap. 'Ah, yes, of course, Mrs Rochester. The famous secret in the attic.'

'Is that what you were looking for?'

Evelyn gave her a puzzled frown. 'I beg your pardon; I'm struggling to understand this conversation.'

Lady Gayle, exasperated, rose, and paced before the fire. *The inspector always makes his questioning look so easy. There's only one thing for it. Be direct.* 'What are you looking for in the attics? You and Sarah are spending a lot of time up there.'

'Are you quite well, Gayle? I haven't spent any time in your attics. Why would I? What are you hiding up there?'

'Nothing.' Lady Gayle put her hands on her hips and stared at Evelyn. 'I must be mistaken. I'm sorry I disturbed you. Please go back to your reading, but if I might ask that you use a bookmark to save your place rather than turning the corner down.'

Evelyn blinked at her, and Lady Gayle, suddenly flushed with embarrassment, rushed from the room.

CHAPTER TWENTY-FIVE

Once back in her bedroom, Lady Gayle rang for Alice and together, the two women headed for the attics. Since it was still daytime, the rooms were infused with a low light. Alice took no chances, however, and lit several candles. Some she left by the door, and the two women took one each and started at the far end of the attic room, opening the trunks, and going through the contents.

There was a veritable jumble of old clothes and papers similar to those Lady Gayle had found before.

'There has to be something here,' Lady Gayle announced, plonking herself down on a nearby trunk. Dust wafted up, and she sneezed.

'Perhaps they found what they wanted and took it with them?' replied Alice. She knelt in front of a trunk and was pulling out sheaf after sheaf of papers.

'That makes sense,' said Lady Gayle. 'When was the last time you heard noises up here?'

'The night before yesterday.'

'Nothing last night?'

'No, milady.'

'Then we may have been beaten to the prize.' Lady Gayle rose from the trunk and looked over Alice's shoulder before she wandered to the door. She returned to her maid's side, looked in the trunk once more and then again at the outside. 'Alice, could you take everything out of that trunk, please?'

Alice frowned but did as she was asked. 'Oh, milady,' she breathed. 'How clever you are. How did you know?'

'It was just a guess really,' replied Lady Gayle modestly. She dropped to the floor by Alice's side, and together, they prodded and poked at the base of the trunk.

'It does sound hollow, milady,' said Alice.

'Yes, but how can we pull it up? We might need a knife to slip down the edge,' replied Lady Gayle in frustration. She sat back, curling her legs beneath her and racking her brains. 'Uncle Percival said there were lots of secrets in this house. He showed me a secret drawer once... oh my goodness. Maybe this trunk has a secret drawer too.' Lady Gayle knelt in front of the trunk, but this time, ran her hands around the outside, touching each of the slats, edge clamps and hasps in turn. Now practically lying on her stomach, she pressed two strap tabs at the same time. There was a soft click, and the hidden compartment popped open.

Alice squealed in excitement as Lady Gayle pulled the drawer open. Inside was a ribbon-bound document and a large iron key. She unravelled the ribbon and opened out the papers. There were several sheets of thick vellum paper. When she brought it closer to the light, she saw it read: The Last Will and Testament of Lord Percival Summer, Earl of Bethencourt.

This is what the searchers had been after—the documents of succession for Bethencourt Castle.

. . .

Lady Gayle woke with a start. Someone was opening the door to her room. She lay silently in the darkened room, scarcely daring to breathe whilst allowing her eyes to become used to the low light. There was a full moon, and the silvery light shone through a gap in the curtains. As her eyes became used to the dimness, she saw a shadow creep across to her dressing table. Are they after my jewels? The shadow tugged at the drawers, which were locked. With a sigh, the person withdrew something from their pocket and jiggled with the lock. Finally, it gave way, and they pulled the drawer open, pushing items in the drawer around as they rifled through the contents. Lady Gayle moved in the bed as if she'd stirred in her sleep. The shadow stiffened, peered towards her bed, and then crept back to the bedroom door and left as silently as they had arrived.

Lady Gayle reached for an eiderdown in the darkness. She wrapped it around her shoulders before she lit her candle. Opening her bedroom door, she placed the candlestick on the small hall table before closing the door as quietly as possible. With the eiderdown held tightly against her neck in one hand and candlestick in the other, she crept along the corridor to the top of the stairs.

The intruder, for surely it could not be someone staying in the castle, sneaked down the stairs and glided across the hall to the library.

Lady Gayle waited until the person had entered the library before scampering down the stairs to listen at the library door. She tried to reach out to open the door, but with both hands full, it was impossible. She dropped the candlestick, and hot wax ran down the eiderdown.

'Blast,' she muttered, but it was too late. No sooner had

she opened the library door than she heard the window on the far side of the room creak open, the grounds outside were lit perfectly by moonbeams. A figure jumped out of the window and down the lawn towards the lake.

Lady Gayle stumbled towards a lamp and switched it on.

The drawers on her desk were open, and papers had been pulled out. She smiled to herself, closed and locked the windows and returned to her bedroom, where she lifted the iron key and the will from under her pillow. Glad that they were safe, she stepped over to the dressing table. Sifting through the sheaf of papers, she realised that some were missing. The thief must have taken them, and Lady Gayle knew what they were after. *At least you had the good sense to keep them safe, but you had better call Mr Southall in the morning.*

Despite her disturbed night, Lady Gayle woke early. She peeked out of the window to see the mist rising in soft clouds from the warming ground. It was going to be a perfect December day. It was far too early to call Mr Southall, so she dressed quickly in her riding habit and made her way to the stables.

If Shepherd was surprised to see her up and about so early, he made no comment but had Billy, the stable lad saddle Plantagenet.

'Have a nice ride, my lady,' he said, tipping his cap.

'Thank you,' she replied and trotted out of the yard. She looked in the direction of the Winterbottom's farm but decided to head cross country away from the border with Colonel Gosforth's land.

She let Plantagenet have his head, feeling her heart

beating faster and faster in time with the thump of his galloping hooves. As she neared the woodland, she eased his pace, and they slowed to a walk. Panting, and with the gelding blowing heavily, she slipped to the ground and led him into the forest. At once, a flock of crows took to the sky, cawing their annoyance that their early morning had been disturbed by her presence. She raised her eyes to the heavens, watching them swirl in the air, dipping and rising until they came to rest once more in the branches of the bare trees.

Their cacophony was not silenced. They were making their distress at her walking through their forest very apparent. Suddenly, they took off, and the woodland fell silent. The absence of sound was eerie, making the hairs on her neck rise. She swallowed hard but pressed on deeper into the woods. Her breathing steadied as woodland sounds returned, the dripping of dew onto leaves and the chirps of small birds. Tiny mammals rustled in the undergrowth, and she drew comfort from the sounds.

After a while, the trees opened out into a clearing. Pale sunlight shone through the gap where the trees were not so close. Light glistened on something metallic, and Lady Gayle stepped closer. It was an old milk urn. It bore rust in places, but other spots shone brightly—spots where bullets had passed through the metal.

She looked around, kicking the leaves away with her booted feet. Here and there, she found other cans, blocks of wood and even small rocks and stones which had been shot at.

It was someone's private target practice range and far enough away from the house that the shots would not be heard. To her mind, that could only mean one person.

Jumping onto a log, she hefted herself onto Plantagenet's back. 'I've got to find out what happened to that boy,' she muttered to herself. 'Perhaps he's trying to hasten his inheritance along?' Determined, she decided to send a message to Mr Southall as soon as she was back inside the castle, regardless of how early it was. Now decided on a course of action, she headed home.

CHAPTER TWENTY-SIX

As she drew closer to the castle, Lady Gayle saw the turrets poking above the trees. A sense of reaching safety overwhelmed her when she saw Evelyn plodding along on Bessie. Lady Gayle called out to her friend, but her voice was lost on the breeze. Evelyn and Bessie continued to plod along, oblivious to the rest of the world. Suddenly, Lady Gayle was gripped by fear. *What if Evelyn is in danger?* Now that she was even more convinced that Mr Howden was behind the death of Lady Sylvia and perhaps even her father; she wondered if, in his madness, he had attacked Colonel Gosforth too.

She decided it would be much easier to gallop to Bessie. Once again, she let the horse have his head, and they cantered down the slope, heading for the gap between two large oaks.

The wind rushed past her face, making her eyes water. She was flying, loving the incredible feeling of the powerful animal racing along. She raised a hand to clear her vision, but suddenly, she felt a jolt, and she was flying over the horse's head. Winded, she lay on the ground. Plantagenet lay beside her, struggling to get to his feet. She crawled over to him.

'Gayle, stay still. You could have broken something,' Evelyn called out as she and Bessie arrived.

Lady Gayle grunted and took off her scarf. She crawled over to Plantagenet and wrapped it around the cut on the horse's leg. This done, she yelled to Evelyn, 'Go and get help!'

White-faced, Evelyn turned Bessie around and trotted towards the stables for help.

'Faster,' yelled Lady Gayle. 'Go faster.' She lay back on the frosty grass, stroking Plantagenet's neck. All the time, she lay on the cold ground thinking about the strange expression she'd seen on Evelyn's face. I'm sure that it's just shock, she told herself.

After lying on the cold ground for a while, Lady Gayle rose. She'd lost all sense of time, not knowing how long she had lain on the grass comforting Plantagenet, but she knew if she didn't move soon, she'd freeze. Wondering what had caused their fall, she edged towards the two oaks and found the cause. Firmly tied between the trees around waist height was a stout rope. She cursed herself, knowing that she'd ridden her horse directly into the trap. Had it been any higher, it would have missed the horse and taken her head off. She groaned. *He's utterly determined to kill me.*

Hearing the calls of Shepherd, she turned away from the rope and saw the head groom, two stable hands, Alice, and Fredericks, making their way towards her. When they reached her, Lady Gayle collapsed into unexpected tears.

'It's the shock,' she heard Fredericks say to Alice. 'Keep her warm and give her some brandy.'

Alice wrapped her in a warm blanket. 'If you can stand up, milady,' she said, 'we'll get you to the car. Mr Chadwick has brought it as close as he can.'

Lady Gayle nodded. 'I want to make sure that Plantagenet is well,' she said.

'He's in good hands, milady,' replied Alice. 'Let Mr Shepherd take care of him, and I'll take care of you.'

As she was led away, Lady Gayle turned back. Shepherd and the stable lads had bound the horse's cut and got him to his feet. The horse, too, was covered in a thick blanket and being led to the horse box, harnessed to old Seamus. Plantagenet limped, gingerly placing his injured leg to the ground. One stable lad was vainly trying to hold the leg off the ground, and the horse struggled towards the box.

As the stable lads eased him up the ramp and into the box, Plantagenet whinnied in pain, and Lady Gayle's heart squeezed. 'I'll never forgive myself,' she said.

'The veterinary surgeon has been telephoned, milady,' said Alice. 'So has Dr Sloane. We just need to get you both back to the castle.'

Lady Gayle allowed herself to be led to the waiting vehicle, tears streaming down her face.

Although she refused to lie down in her room, Lady Gayle went there to change her clothes and be examined by the doctor while Alice sat calmly by her side. Having been given a clean bill of health, although told to rest and not exert herself, Lady Gayle ate the sandwiches Alice had brought her on a tray.

'Please sit down, Alice. We need to talk,' said her ladyship.

Alice gave her a concerned look but did as she was bid.

'Before I came off Plantagenet, I found a spot in the

woods that someone has been using for target practice,' she said. 'I think the shooter is Mr Howden.'

'Mr Howden? But he seems such a nice young man,' replied Alice. 'Not a gentleman, of course, but very nice all the same.'

'Mr Howden wears glasses and didn't do military service.'

'I don't think he likes guns, milady. Mr Fredericks says even when he was invited to shoot pheasants, he always found an excuse.'

'Alice, someone broke into my room last night,' continued her ladyship. 'They didn't get anything, but then they escaped through the library windows. So, it can't have been anyone staying in the house.'

'Are you sure? They may have gone that way simply to put you off the scent.'

'I'm sure,' said Lady Gayle with a grim smile. 'I also found Mr Howden looking at the portrait of Uncle Percival last week.'

'He was very fond of the old man, at least, that's the gossip in the servants' hall. The old man was fond of him, too. And your father liked him. I can't believe that he's the one.'

'Who else could it be?' asked Lady Gayle.

Alice dipped her head. 'I really couldn't say, milady.' She rose. 'If that's everything? Mrs Mitchell asked if I could help serve lunch today.'

Lady Gayle tilted her head to the side. 'Is Owens seeking a new position?' she said.

'Yes, milady,' replied Alice before she dashed out of the room, leaving her ladyship to ponder some more over Mr Howden's behaviour.

. . .

Mr Southall arrived after lunch. Fredericks showed him into the library, and after giving him time to read through the documents she had found, Lady Gayle joined him.

'What have you uncovered?' she asked, popping the telegram that Fredericks handed her onto the table.

'Well, it's as we thought, my lady. There was a son on your great uncle's side, something like a fourth cousin to you. He was named Hillary Summer, but I have investigated army records, and he died at the Somme.'

'And there are no other claimants?'

Mr Southall drew in a deep breath. He looked reluctant to speak, as if he needed to choose his words extremely carefully. 'It has,' he began, 'been compulsory to register a child's birth since 1875. Made law under the Births and Deaths Act of 1874...'

'Yes,' said Lady Gayle impatiently. 'Go on.'

'Hillary Summer's birth in 1896 was registered and is recorded by the General Register Office. His death in 1918 was recorded there too. However, there was another birth, and that has only just come to light.'

'There was another child? Who? Is he still alive?'

'This child was born in 1898. There is some mention in family letters, but I haven't managed to track down a birth certificate.'

'Hasn't it been recorded by this... this General Register Office?'

'It would appear not.' Mr Southall sighed again. 'I have used a private detective to search the register, and he has not been able to find the child's birth. It could be that the child wasn't registered, but the parents would have been liable for prosecution if so.'

'Where does all this leave us? Is there another claimant or not? If they were born in 1898, that makes them twenty-four. Two years younger than me. Being older, does that make my claim stronger?' Lady Gayle rose and paced in front of the fire. 'Where are the family letters? Could someone have written to Great Uncle Percival?'

'Perhaps. He may even have recorded the birth in the family bible.'

Lady Gayle remembered the huge book. Uncle Percival had shown it to her once when she was very young. 'I remember seeing it, but I have not seen it for years. I don't know if it is here or if it's in the chapel.'

'I have spent some time looking for it here in the library, but to no avail. I had forgotten about the chapel. Lord Percival stopped using it after Maxwell, Viscount Bethencourt, was killed. Shall we go there now, my lady?'

Lady Gayle nodded and made for the door. As she opened the library door, she heard feet scuttling away.

CHAPTER TWENTY-SEVEN

SHE PULLED THE DOOR WIDE OPEN, BUT THE HALLWAY WAS EMPTY other than Fredericks appearing through the baize-covered door which led to the kitchen stairs.

'We're going to the chapel, Fredericks,' she said.

'Very good, my lady,' replied Fredericks with his usual half-bow. 'Will you require a coat? It is very cold outside.'

Lady Gayle nodded and then waited impatiently for coats to be fetched. Although it would have been no quicker if she had collected her own coat, it was the standing around feeling useless that she hated. Mr Southall quickly wrapped himself up for the frosty weather; his hat jammed firmly on his head.

The intrepid pair left by the front door and marched across towards the chapel, frozen grass crunching under their boots.

As Lady Gayle had expected, the chapel was locked. She brought the large iron key out of her pocket and tried it in the lock. 'I found it with the documents I gave you,' she said in response to the solicitor's frown.

He nodded, and they stepped over the threshold. Inside,

the chapel was as cold as the day outside, and their breath frosted as they walked towards the lectern. It was empty. The bible they had expected to see there was nowhere to be seen.

Lady Gayle gritted her teeth. 'It has to be here somewhere,' she said. 'It's not in the house.'

'Perhaps your uncle hid it?' suggested Mr Southall.

'Perhaps,' responded Lady Gayle, 'but where? Come on, Uncle Percival. Where did you hide it?' She gazed around the small chapel, shivering in the chill. Closing her eyes, she thought back to her childhood games and playing with her brother and cousins in the castle grounds and buildings. Then she remembered.

'There was a priest hole,' she said. 'The castle had been a royalist enclave before it was given into Cromwellian hands. Catholicism was illegal, and it was only by chance that the chapel wasn't destroyed entirely. Rupert found the secret one summer. We kept it from Uncle Percival, but I think he already knew. Here.' She pulled the damp, mildewed altar cloth aside and pressed the centre of the carved coat of arms that lay beneath. A small door popped open, and inside what would have been a very cramped interior for a grown man to hide in, sat a large leather-bound tome. Lady Gayle reached in and pulled it from its hiding place. She placed it on the altar and opened it up.

The family bible of the original owners of Bethencourt Castle lay before them.

Lady Gayle carefully turned the pages to the family record at the front of the bible and ran her finger down the list of names.

'There's nothing here,' she said, turning to Mr Southall. 'Look, there's Maxwell, Alfred, me and then Rupert. There are no other children. Certainly not this Hillary you found. We're the last entries.'

'Most odd,' said Mr Southall. He removed his owlish spectacles and polished them. 'Where are the deaths recorded?'

Lady Gayle flipped the births page over and inspected the list of deaths. The ink inscription recording Maxwell's and Rupert's deaths was as bright as if it had been written in the previous few days rather than eight years ago. 'I suppose we should record Father's death too,' she murmured, batting a tear away. 'I'll need a new page.' She turned the page expecting to find a blank deaths page, but instead, scrawled in an impatient hand were two names. Hillary Summer, and the name of his sister. Evelyn.

'Evelyn?' whispered Lady Gayle. 'What a strange coincidence. It can't possibly be Miss Trent. She's my friend.'

'How long have you known her?' said Mr Southall.

'Since... since before Hugh died. She was a new recruit. She'd requested a posting to our unit, which we all thought was madness as we were right at the front. The work was very dangerous.'

'How did she find out you were there?' Mr Southall had replaced his glasses and was peering at the bible.

'Mama and Papa put an engagement announcement in *The Times*. Then there was a little article about wartime weddings, and we were included in that too...'

'I see,' replied the solicitor. 'Well, I suggest we take this back into the library, where it's warmer and where we can talk to Evelyn Trent and hear her side of the story.' Mr Southall closed the bible and hefted it from the altar.

Her ladyship closed its hiding place, and together, they retraced their steps to the library where warmth, refreshments, and the truth awaited them.

CHAPTER TWENTY-EIGHT

Once in the library, Mr Southall laid the ancient bible on the large table, and Lady Gayle called for her butler.

'Could you ask Miss Trent to join us, please, Fredericks?' she said. 'And could you ask Alice to join us too?'

'I am sorry, my lady, but Miss Trent went to the village. She had an urgent letter to post. I was expecting her back some time ago, but she must have been delayed.'

Lady Gayle glanced at Mr Southall and raised her eyebrows. 'Bring Sarah Snodgrass here then. She may know something. Those two have been as thick as thieves since Evelyn got here.'

Fredericks bowed his head and left the room. A few minutes later, he returned with the maid Sarah. She seemed reluctant to enter, and Fredericks placed a hand on her shoulder to guide her into the room in front of him. Alice followed the pair into the library.

'I don't know anything,' Sarah said.

'I rather think that you do, Sarah,' replied Lady Gayle. 'Please sit down. You too, Alice.'

Both maids exchanged glances but pulled chairs close to the table.

Lady Gayle paced in front of the fire. 'How long have you known Evelyn Trent, Sarah?'

'Miss Evelyn? Only since she came to stay here, milady.' Sarah pulled a rag from her apron pocket and blew her nose.

'That's a lie, Sarah. And I can prove it.' Lady Gayle picked up the telegram she'd received earlier. She opened it and placed it on the table with a flourish. 'This telegram came from Cracknell's in Bond Street at lunchtime. It didn't make sense at first because the order for the roses came from Bethencourt Castle, with the request that they were to be sent urgently with no card. I think you placed that order, Sarah.'

The miserable maid bowed her head, shaking it from side to side. 'I didn't,' she said.

'You were here, Sarah. With your mistress, Lady Sylvia. Tell me, did you plan for her to die, or was the shot intended for me?'

Sarah remained mute.

'And what were you doing in the attics? What was the idea there? What were you looking for?'

Sarah raised her head and glowered at Lady Gayle, who took a step towards the miserable creature before her. 'Come along, Sarah, we know most of it. You're just filling in the gaps.'

'You know what we were looking for. You've got it there.' She pointed at the bible. 'Miss Evelyn wanted to see her name in it. To prove she was next in line.'

'But how would she inherit if she'd been hung for Lady Sylvia's murder? Or mine for that matter?'

'That's where her plan was so good, you see. She killed

Lady Sylvia, but you were going to be found guilty. You'd be hung, then she'd find the bible and inherit.'

'And when that failed?'

'Then she knew she had to get rid of you,' said Sarah. 'She—' There was a sharp retort from near the window, and Sarah fell to the floor. Her eyes remained open, blood spreading onto the rug from a wound on the side of her head.

Fredericks rushed into the room while Mr Southall stepped quickly to the window and pushed the curtains aside. The window was open, but there was no one in sight.

'Dash it all,' snapped Lady Gayle. 'Fredericks, get the men together. Go after her. She can't have got far.'

'My lady,' replied Fredericks. He called Gaspod, and they left the room.

Lady Gayle collapsed in a chair, head in hands. 'It seems Evelyn befriended me under false pretences,' she said. 'How could I have been so stupid? Well done, Alice. You saw through her.'

'I should have mentioned it before, milady...' Alice began. 'When we were in the post office, I saw Miss Evelyn coming out of the ironmongers. She had a basket. I thought I saw a coil of rope, but then I decided my eyes were playing tricks on me, and I decided not to say anything.'

'Yes, she must have laid that trap for me and Plantagenet too. However, Alice, even if you had told me, I'm not sure that it would have made any difference,' replied Lady Gayle. She smiled at Alice. 'There's every chance that I wouldn't have believed you, isn't there?'

'Perhaps, milady. But I'd be happier if I had mentioned it all the same.'

Lady Gayle gave her a brief nod. 'It doesn't matter. We

know everything now.' She glanced at the door as Fredericks entered.

'I have gathered the men, my lady. Mr Shepherd has the bloodhound, and they are on her trail as we speak. She won't get far. I have also taken the liberty of sending Owens for the local constable. He should arrive soon.'

'And now we wait,' said Lady Gayle, tapping her foot. 'Patience is not my forte. I'm going to the stables to see how Plantagenet is faring.'

She swept from the room, gathering her coat and hat as she went.

As Lady Gayle trudged to the stables, she ran over everything that had happened over the past few weeks. The atmosphere of Bethencourt Castle had changed dramatically from her childhood memories of the place. She pulled up her collar and looked over her shoulder, wondering where the gunman had run to.

Quickening her pace, she realised how stupid leaving the comparative safety of the castle had been. She ran into the stable yard, straight into the head groom.

'My lady,' he said, 'are you quite well?'

'I'm just being silly, Shepherd,' she said. 'I wanted to see Plantagenet, and I rushed out here, and then I realised...'

Shepherd gave her a puzzled frown. 'The horse is fine, your ladyship. I was just about to change his dressing. Perhaps you could wait in the tack room or the feed store while I do that?'

Lady Gayle smiled wistfully. 'There was a time, Mr Shepherd,' she said, 'when I would have done that happily, but I can't help but think this is all my fault. I'll come with you. I'll even help if you'll let me.'

She followed the groom to the gelding's loose box and sat on an upturned bucket while Shepherd unwrapped the bandage on Plantagenet's leg. The cut was puffy and sore looking, but it was clean, and there was no puss on the old dressing.

'He'll have a scar, milady, not unlike yourself, but he'll live.' Shepherd smeared ointment onto a fresh dressing and applied it to the horse's leg. Plantagenet nuzzled him and whinnied softly.

'My lady.' Fredericks's voice over the door to the loose box sounded panicked. 'We were worried. I think you should come back to the house. Mr Shepherd, I'll need a couple of stout lads to accompany us.'

If Mr Shepherd was at all puzzled, he didn't show it. He simply cleaned up the used dressings and called Billy. Together, they surrounded Lady Gayle and escorted her safely back to the castle.

CHAPTER TWENTY-NINE

Despite the best efforts of the searchers, they returned empty-handed after several hours. Even Gaspod had lost the trail.

'The men will try again in the morning, my lady,' Fredericks reported. 'Mr Shepherd thinks she must have crossed several streams to put the dog off her scent.'

'Yes, that makes sense,' replied Lady Gayle. 'Has everyone retired for the evening?'

'Everyone except yourself, my lady.'

'And you,' replied her ladyship. 'I think we should both call it a night, Fredericks.'

'As you wish, my lady.'

Lady Gayle trudged up to her room, loosening her hair as she opened the door. A figure was hunched over her writing desk.

'Evelyn, how did you get in? What on earth are you doing here? Everyone is searching for you. Why are you here in my room?'

Evelyn turned away from the writing desk, levelling the small pistol at her old friend. 'I suppose it's all over now,' she said.

'It is,' replied Lady Gayle, her eyes flicking from the gun to Evelyn's face. 'I know everything: how you found me, how you befriended me while all the time you were lying to my face. Tell me, Evelyn, what was your plan?'

'I had Sarah send a message to call you back to the house. I knew you'd not stop Lady Sylvia from having fun. You like to think you are so unselfish, don't you? I shot her when you had no alibi and no excuse for leaving her to ride out alone.'

'No alibi? I was here in the house working on estate accounts. You can ask any of the servants.'

'Loyal servants. I took the risk that a jury would believe they were lying for you,' Evelyn said with a sneer. She stepped away from the writing desk, holding up a sheaf of papers in her left hand. 'I had every right to look at these papers,' she snarled.

Lady Gayle drew her eyebrows together with the flicker of a frown. 'Yes, I suppose you do,' she said. 'But no one knew you existed. Not until we saw those letters and your name in the bible.'

Evelyn Trent squinted at the papers. 'Yes, everyone assumed there was just one child. However, as you have discovered, there were two. Hillary was registered, and the other child, a girl, me, well, my birth was simply noted in the family bible. I was not a boy and so not important enough.'

'I'm sorry, Evelyn.' Lady Gayle meant it, but she thought back over her entire history with Evelyn Trent. Their chance encounter in France and then again after the war, meeting up once more in London just after Uncle Percival's death.

Nothing was chance or coincidental. Nothing was by accident. Everything was by design. Lady Gayle clenched her fists.

'Have you finally worked it all out, Countess Bethencourt?' Evelyn sneered.

'I think so,' said Lady Gayle. 'You must have started looking for me some time ago.'

'I started as soon as your brother and cousins were killed,' replied Evelyn. 'That's when I realised it was only you and your father who stood between me, my brother and all this.' She waved her arms to indicate the room and all its trappings.

Lady Gayle nodded. Whilst they had been talking, she'd edged herself closer to the bedroom door. With her hands behind her back, she removed the large key from the lock, hoping that she didn't drop it on the floor. Evelyn was so engrossed in her own triumph that she didn't seem to notice.

'I see.' Lady Gayle nodded. 'Mr Southall said that your brother had been killed in 1918. Almost as the fighting was coming to an end.'

Evelyn whimpered like an animal in pain. 'He was so close to surviving. Only a few more weeks, but he wasn't killed in action but by the influenza.'

'I'm so sorry,' replied Lady Gayle. She grasped the door key, the iron cold against her warm hands. She eased it out of the lock and twisted the doorknob. If she could escape the room, then she could imprison Evelyn until the police came. She pulled the door open, and the hinges squeaked, sounding as loud as cannon fire in the silent room. Lady Gayle flung the door open and rushed through it, pulling it shut behind her. Her hands shook as she tried to insert the cumbersome key into the lock. She was just about to turn it when Evelyn wrenched the door open.

Lady Gayle took one look at Evelyn's face and snatched the vase of flowers from the hall table. She flung them at Evelyn, knocking the gun from her hands. It skittered under the large bed. Then she raced down the corridor, hoping that Evelyn wouldn't be able to retrieve the gun. At the top of the stairs, she tripped and fell to the ground. Evelyn, unarmed, launched herself at Lady Gayle and pinned her down.

Lady Gayle felt her face being pushed into the carpet, and she twisted around, trying to buck her assailant off.

Evelyn pulled her hair, and Lady Gayle squealed in pain. Momentarily blinded by her tears, Lady Gayle twisted again, trying to get her back flat against the floor so she could clutch Evelyn's hands and stop the hair pulling.

It was not perhaps her best idea, and Evelyn knelt on her spine, pressing her knees into her lungs, trying to asphyxiate her. Lady Gayle pushed herself to her elbows, bringing her knees up beneath her. She braced herself, remembering the games of horsey with her brother. Alfred always managed to buck her off. *Can I do that?* With one strong movement, she curled her toes up and pushed, desperately scrabbling to get her feet in place. She bucked Evelyn from her back and onto the floor. She crouched, then launched herself at the dazed Evelyn. But Evelyn had not given in. She pushed herself from the floor, and with her fingers curled into talons, she launched herself at Lady Gayle. The two women tugged at each other's hair, screeching like banshees.

Below, Lady Gayle heard running feet on the marble flooring. Regardless of the late hour, help would soon be at hand.

Evelyn was not giving in easily, however, and Lady Gayle wheezed when she felt the bannister rail collide with her hip bone. She stumbled on the staircase, one foot giving way underneath her as she missed her footing. She closed her eyes, trying to relax her body as she would if she were falling from a horse. She knew if she stiffened up, she might not live through the tumble down the stairs. On the cusp of falling into oblivion, she felt a tug on her leg and hit her head on a stair tread.

Evelyn was not so lucky. With a terrified scream, she tumbled head over heels down the stairs, finally coming to rest on the marble floor below.

Lady Gayle sat at the top of the stairs with Alice, her rescuer, and the two women watched the crimson pool as it surrounded Evelyn's head.

In the hallway below, Fredericks appeared and swiftly had the situation under control. The village policeman was already expected while Fredericks stood over Evelyn's body, fussing about the blood and the damage to the marble flooring.

'Nonsense,' replied the Dowager Countess. 'It will continue the castle's bloody past.'

From their vantage point at the top of the stairs, they didn't miss Fredericks' theatrical shudder.

'I'm suddenly very tired,' said Lady Gayle.

'I think a nice strong cup of tea is in order,' said Alice. 'I'll help you to your room for a lie down and then go to the kitchen for you.'

'You're a lifesaver,' said Lady Gayle, knowing Alice had literally saved her life. Had she fallen too, instead of Evelyn, it could have been her lying in a pool of her own blood on the cold marble floor.

Once Alice had made her comfortable and warm in her room, Lady Gayle finally gave in to the shock and allowed the tears to roll unchecked down her face.

By the time Alice returned with a tray of tea and ginger biscuits—which Cook insisted were good for shock and nausea. Lady Gayle had dried her eyes and gathered up the papers Evelyn had been so anxious to read.

CHAPTER THIRTY

Lady Gayle patted Plantagenet and fed him a carrot. The grey munched contentedly and rubbed his muzzle against her jacket.

'Is he getting better?'

Lady Gayle whirled around at the sound of the voice. Mr Howden stood before her; he was twisting his hat in his hands. She frowned. *What else does he want to say?*

'Before you say anything,' she said. 'I have something I need to say.'

'My lady,' he replied. He replaced his hat and tilted his head to one side.

'An apology,' she began, choosing to ignore the smirk that flickered across his face. 'I suspected you of being the killer. I did for a long time, and it... well, it stopped me from seeing the truth.'

'I see,' Mr Howden said. 'Is that it?'

'How do you mean?' she said.

'Is that my apology?'

'Ah, yes, of course. Mr Howden, I humbly apologise and beg your forgiveness.'

'Granted.' He smiled and held out his hand.

Lady Gayle shook it firmly and accompanied him back to the little Austin. She tutted when she saw the pool of oil under the car again.

'You really should get that sorted,' she said.

Mr Howden shrugged. 'I tried myself, but I only seemed to make it worse.'

'Do you know about engines, Mr Howden?' Lady Gayle asked.

Mr Howden shook his head. 'I don't,' he replied. 'And I do wish you'd call me Harry. Your uncle did.'

'I will think about it,' Lady Gayle said. 'Wait there.'

She wandered across the stable yard to where Chadwick was cleaning the Bentley. After a brief chat, Chadwick went to the loose box where he kept some tools. He loaded a few in a wheelbarrow with a canister of oil, which he trundled towards the land agent's car.

'Mr Chadwick, honestly, it's fine,' said Mr Howden. 'I will take it to the garage in the village.'

Chadwick raised his eyebrows, touched his cap to her ladyship and returned to his work on the Bentley.

Lady Gayle rolled up her sleeves and covered her clothes with the brown apron that Chadwick had placed in the wheelbarrow. With sleeve covers over her blouse, she opened the bonnet and went to work.

Mr Howden stood in silence as she worked on the engine. When her ladyship placed a wheeled board on the floor, he began to protest but was silenced by a single glance. She lay on the board and rolled herself under the car, shouting instructions to Mr Howden about the tools she required.

After a while, she rolled out from under the car, opened the oil reservoir and poured in the fresh oil supplied by the chauffeur. Finally satisfied, Lady Gayle rubbed her hands on a cloth.

'It should be fine now.' She looked at the land agent. 'Give it a try. Then you can move the car, and we can clean up this mess.'

Mr Howden sat behind the wheel and turned the engine over. He reversed the little car and pulled it into a new spot. When he turned the engine off, Lady Gayle was already standing waiting with a bucketful of sand. He took it from her and shook it over the oil which he'd leaked on the cobbles. Putting the bucket on the ground, he removed his handkerchief from his pocket and passed it to Lady Gayle.

She gave him a quizzical look, and he indicated on his face where the smudge of oil was on hers.

She took the handkerchief and dabbed at her cheek while he smiled at her attempts to rid herself of the dirty mark.

'Oh, you do it,' she said, thrusting the handkerchief at him.

He took it from her, wrapped the end around his index finger, and then, very carefully, he wiped the streak of oil from Lady Gayle's face.

CHAPTER THIRTY-ONE

Lady Gayle Summer followed her mother up the few steps into the hallway of Bethencourt Castle. She removed her thick black winter coat and cloche hat, handing both to Alice.

'How was the service, milady?' said Alice.

'Rather lovely,' replied her ladyship. 'I think I finally feel ready for Christmas.'

'It's been quite a year,' replied her mother. 'Will you join me in the drawing room, Gayle? I have something for you.'

Lady Gayle raised her eyebrows and winked at her maid, causing the young woman to giggle. She soon stopped when the Dowager Countess glanced at her.

Fredericks opened the door, and the countesses wandered into the room towards the fire. The motley crew of dogs thumped their tails but didn't move away from the heat.

'It's there.' The Dowager Countess pointed to a large box on the floor by the massive tree. It was covered in wrapping paper from the House of Hermès, Paris.

Lady Gayle frowned at her mother in surprise. 'What on earth can it be?'

'There is only one way to find out, Gayle,' replied her mother.

Lady Gayle knelt on the floor and carefully removed the wrapping paper. Then she opened the box. The smell of new leather hit her immediately, and she pulled the box apart to find a new saddle. Not a side saddle. One where she could sit astride the horse—like a man.

'Oh, Mama,' Lady Gayle breathed. 'It's beautiful. You shouldn't have, but why?'

'You told me that I had to move with the times, and I've decided that you are right. I know you find a riding habit cumbersome and prefer breeches, and now you can ride any way that you like.'

'Thank you, Mama.' Lady Gayle's eyes misted, and she brushed a tear away.

'Now, now,' said her mother. 'Decorum, remember.'

'Yes, Mama. Of course.' Her ladyship rose, however, and went to the sofa where her mother was seated and kissed her on the cheek.

'Don't make a fuss, dear,' said the Dowager Countess. 'We need to talk.'

Lady Gayle tilted her head. 'We do?'

'Yes, about the running of the house and the estate.'

'Mama? You're not going to talk about money, are you?'

'Don't be ridiculous. What on earth gave you that idea?' Lady Ethel drew a plain white lace handkerchief from her bag and dabbed at her nose.

Where's the black lace? thought Lady Gayle, realising that her gift to her mother of a dozen lace-trimmed handkerchiefs may not be suitable.

'I have simply decided that you are right about running

everything. You can't do it all, and so I have decided that I will do as you asked, and I will take on the running of the house and the domestic staff. You can continue with the outside staff and the estate.

'I know you don't want to find a new husband, but I do think you should consider the future of the estate. You are going to need to leave it to someone.'

Lady Gayle backed away to sit on the sofa opposite her mother. *It's now or never.* 'I'm not sure if I can have another baby,' she began.

Her mother gave her a sharp glance; her mouth opened, but no words came.

'I lost my baby when I was told about Hugh's death. I didn't know I was expecting.' Lady Gayle bit back a sob, and Molly jumped onto the sofa beside her, placing her paws on Lady Gayle's knees. Fondling the dog's silky ears, Lady Gayle continued her explanation to her mother. 'I was told that I should be able to have a baby in the future, but I missed Hugh and didn't want a replacement. I still don't.'

'Oh, Gayle, you should have told me. Why did you keep this from me for so long? Did you tell your father? You and he were so close. I can't believe you kept it from him too.'

'I didn't want to see the pity in your eyes. Or Papa's. It was bad enough without Hugh. I couldn't bear to face what else I'd lost.'

'Did you not think I would understand? I have lost a child too,' said Lady Ethel.

'Perhaps that's why I said nothing. We'd all lost so much. I was only a few weeks gone. Too soon to know.' Molly whimpered, and Lady Gayle pulled the dog onto her lap for a cuddle.

'Know?' asked her mother.

'If it was a boy or a girl,' replied Lady Gayle.

Lady Ethel dipped her head. She didn't respond for a moment. She held her Yorkshire Terrier close to her chest. Then she said, 'It may not be appropriate, but I have asked Mr Howden to dine with us. Your Great Uncle Percival was so fond of him and treated him as if he were family. Your father thought he was a good man, and it seemed like a nice idea if we carried on where Percival left off. I'm sorry I didn't know what you've just told me earlier. I am afraid that I cannot put him off now.'

'That's fine, Mama,' Lady Gayle replied. 'I did have a gift for him. However, I've given it to him already.'

There were noises in the hallway, and Mrs Gosforth was escorted into the drawing room by Mr Howden. Colonel Gosforth had declined his invitation, claiming that he was still confined to his bed under strict orders from Doctor Sloane. Although she thought his decision was based on embarrassment over his accident, since it was Christmas, Lady Gayle decided to give him the benefit of the doubt.

How the only bachelor in the room was going to manage was anyone's guess.

The End

Please flip the page for a note on spellings used by this British author

To my lovely readers,

A very long time ago, I was born in Britain. I love this little island and all its quirks. There are some things that I don't love, but they will never be in the Cassie Rush books.

I tend to use UK English spellings, punctuation, and grammar, including the "u" in colour, humour, rigour, and other words I can't think of right now. I also use an "s" where Americans tend to prefer a "z", such as cosy/cozy. In fact, my laptop just auto-corrected cozy!

I read a vast number of cosy mysteries written by American writers. I love the sarcasm, humour and I especially love the paranormal, witchy novels. It's also made me acutely aware of how the grammar differs between the two languages. It still jars when I read something like, "The dress fit perfectly" instead of, what to me is the correct form, "The dress fit**ted** perfectly", but I know it's different, not wrong.

I hope you'll forgive me for sticking with the language I've been using all my life.

Thanks,
Cassie
Suffolk, UK
April 2023

REVIEWS

I do hope you enjoyed your first meeting with Lady Gayle Summer, Countess Bethencourt.

If so I wonder if you would be so kind as to leave me a review on Amazon or Goodreads?

For paperback readers, please look out for the review request email.

Please join my newsletter here, if you would like to keep in touch, and hear news about my upcoming books and latest releases

Thank you,
Cassie

ACKNOWLEDGMENTS

Getting a book ready for publication is a huge team effort and I'm lucky to be surrounded by such supportive friends and dedicated professionals to make my books the best they can be.

To my fabulous beta team (Patricia, Shelli, Heidi) who gave me such great feedback after the rewrite. Honestly, I could not have done this without you.

To Nola Li Barr who did the final run through. Thank you so much, Nola. You helped me believe again.

To the fabulous Molly Burton who creates the fabulous covers for the Lady Gayle Summer series, the Eastwold-by-the-Sea series and for the Kim David series that will be out very soon.

Finally, a thanks to the launch team, who read through and helped catch the Hide-and-Seek universal champions – the typo. If you find any, let me know. I hate them as much as you do.

Thanks
Cassie
Suffolk 2023

Also by Cassie Rush

Eastwold by the Sea Series

Raising the Roof

Literary Murder

On the Stroke of Death

A Slice of Murder

Lady Gayle Summer series

Summers Slain

Summer Knights

Summer Secrets

Coming soon — Summer Races. The flat racing season has begun, and Lord Ridgewell has bought himself a racehorse. What could possibly go wrong?

ABOUT THE AUTHOR

Hi there, my name is Cassie Rush and I'm a British author of cosy mysteries set in the English country- or seaside.

I absolutely love the coastal town of Southwold which is a short drive up the coast from where I live. It's why I chose to set my popular, Eastwold by the Sea series there. Although my version of the town is entirely fictional as I like to move streets around. I hate it when an author sets a story somewhere you know well and gets details wrong, don't you?

I have been a fan of Agatha Christie all my life and I adore the other golden age authors. I especially enjoy the stories of Miss Marple, Father Brown, Brother Cadfael and Lord Peter Wimsey.

I was really lucky at school (let's not talk about how long ago that was though) to have brilliant and enthusiastic history teachers. It's given me a lifelong love of history and all the tales that the past has to offer.

I also write as Caroline Goldsworthy—these books are rather darker with more graphic content.

Printed in Great Britain
by Amazon

34758960R00111